She'd never dreamt of begging a man to make love to her.

But right now, with Piers, Emma was so close. Her face suffusing with heat, she dipped her head to shield her hungry gaze before it betrayed her. 'I'm not going with you, Piers. It would—it would be wrong.'

'Wrong for who?' Suddenly Piers had to touch her. He drew his fingers gently down the softly velvet surface of her cheek, tipping up her chin so that she was forced to look at him. The pupils of her distinct honey-brown eyes had grown arrestingly dark, and he saw her delicious plump lower lip quiver slightly. Heat exploded inside him like a small inc...

'You need taking care of.'

'No, I don't.'

'Good God, wom... ...argue with me the whole ...

There were other thin... ...ma would much prefer to do with him a... night long, but she had neither the confidence nor the strength to state them. Not with his nearness making it hard for her to take a breath, let alone talk.

The day **Maggie Cox** saw the film version of *Wuthering Heights*, with a beautiful Merle Oberon and a very handsome Laurence Olivier, was the day that she became hooked on romance. From that day onwards she spent a lot of time dreaming up her own romances, secretly hoping that one day she might become published and get paid for doing what she loves most! Now that her dream is being realised, she wakes up every morning and counts her blessings. She is married to a gorgeous man, is the mother of two wonderful sons, and her two other great passions in life—besides her family and reading/writing—are music and films.

Recent titles by the same author:

THE WEALTHY MAN'S WAITRESS

BY
MAGGIE COX

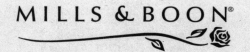
MILLS & BOON®

To Bob and Simone.
I am indebted to you both for love, healing
and the great gift of your friendship

*First published in Great Britain 2004
Harlequin Mills & Boon Limited,
Eton House, 18-24 Paradise Road, Richmond, Surrey TW9 1SR*

© Maggie Cox 2004

ISBN 0 263 83790 4

*Set in Times Roman 10½ on 12 pt.
01-1104-53793*

*Printed and bound in Spain
by Litografia Rosés, S.A., Barcelona*

CHAPTER ONE

THERE was just a door between Emma Jane Robards and her current goal. Only it wasn't just any old common or garden door. No: this one was sleek and forbidding, made out of the finest grained walnut, with a sign in perfectly formed gold lettering that seemed to haughtily announce the name of its occupant like a VIP at a banquet. *Piers Redfield.* Even the name seemed imbued with importance.

'Don't bother trying to arrange an appointment to see him,' Lawrence had advised. 'He employs an army of staff to keep out the riff-raff. No offence.' He'd smiled apologetically and Emma's stomach had churned a little queasily. What on earth was she letting herself in for, sneaking around trying to get into some corporate wizard's protected enclave as if she was some kind of amateur spy or something? And why, oh, why had she allowed Lawrence to even persuade her to consider it?

Because he needed her help, Emma reminded herself with renewed determination, and that was why she was willing to risk being thrown out into the street by Security or—worse—being driven off in a police car. Doggedly tilting her chin to shake off her fear, she rapped her knuckles smartly against the imposing walnut, frankly stunned that she had managed to get as far as the great man's door without being stopped. But today, for once, luck seemed to be on her side.

'Come!'

Into the lion's den… Her thoughts racing, Emma twisted the brass doorknob and swept into the inner sanctum so appropriately guarded by that imposing door, then came to a nervous standstill almost as soon as her feet crossed the threshold. She hadn't expected the room to be quite so huge or awe-inspiring but, with its panoramic windows and endless sea of forest-green carpet, it was. And those beautiful paintings on the walls weren't prints either. They had to be the real thing—even Emma's untrained eye could see that. But more than her intimidating surroundings, or the pervading aura of wealth that hung like exclusive perfume on the air, what commanded her attention the most was the immaculately attired glowering male sitting behind a stylish desk so huge it wouldn't have looked out of place accommodating a small dinner party. Piers Redfield himself.

'Who the hell are you?'

Emma's feet wanted to run, but sheer strength of will made them stay right where they were. Now she'd come this far, she wasn't about to bolt like some frightened rabbit just because he was the head of a hugely successful corporation, a multimillionaire if Lawrence was to be believed, and she a mere waitress in her friend's bistro. He had a lifestyle about a million miles away from her own and probably wouldn't give her the time of day if their paths should ever cross in the normal course of events, but even so, Emma told herself, she had to seize the moment and not be scared. Though in the normal course of events their paths would never cross—probably not even in her wildest dreams. Lawrence hadn't exaggerated. Piers Redfield looked as if he could put the fear of God into just about anyone.

'Are you going to answer me or do I get Security to come and throw you out?' His bellow bounced off the walls and Emma gripped the black leather briefcase she'd brought with her to help her look as if she was meant to be in the building and prayed hard that her bravado would hold out.

'I'm Emma. I'm a friend of Lawrence.'

'Lawrence?' Dark blond brows came together over penetrating blue eyes the seductive hue of an azure sky over the French Riviera. Staring into them, even from this distance, Emma almost forgot the reason she'd come. Unlocking her hand from its death grip on the briefcase handle, she wondered if it was normal for a heart to beat so deafeningly loud, or for fear to grip her courage by the throat and strangle it into oblivion.

'Your son.'

'I know perfectly well he's my son, but that still doesn't explain your presence here. And, while we're on the subject, how did you get past Reception and my assistant without being seen?'

'They're out front watching the Lord Mayor's Show. And I suppose there aren't many people here on a Saturday morning.' When Emma had emerged from the tube station to find herself swept up in the crowd of people thronging the streets, she had prayed with all her might that the occupants of the office buildings lining the route would be distracted by the procession. She'd hardly been able to believe it when she'd found that to be the case. It was a miracle but she had been able to whip past the temporarily empty security desk downstairs as easily as a magician's assistant. *Now you see me, now you don't.*

'Is that on today?'

Without waiting for Emma's confirmation, Piers pushed back his chair and strode over to the window. The way he carried himself was compelling, Emma mused silently, and she couldn't recall ever being fascinated by the way a man moved before. There was a strength and grace about him that put her in mind of an athlete. He probably worked hard to keep himself in prime physical condition. But right then she wished she wouldn't notice such distracting things. There was a very good reason why she was here, and she wasn't going to be put off by Piers Redfield's intimidating good looks, or the fact that wealth and power were obviously second nature to the man. His whole personality radiated those very considerable attributes, and Emma had been amply forewarned by Lawrence that he was a tricky customer not averse to using his extremely potent assets to bend the will of even the most steadfast individual. Well, he wasn't going to get the chance to bend *her* will. As far as Lawrence was concerned, Emma was a woman on a mission.

'You won't see much from there. You're too high up.' Her comment could just as soon have been meant metaphorically. His status certainly put him on a pedestal way above her.

'So much for security. Now, what's this all about? Did Lawrence send you? Who are you—one of his girlfriends?'

One of his girlfriends. The insult was a poisoned barb, clearly meant to sting. Beneath the fitted cerise jacket that she'd reluctantly donned for the occasion over a midlength black skirt, Emma's shoulders stiffened. 'I like to think I mean a little bit more to him than that.' As soon as the words were out she wished she could take them back. Now Piers's lips—those perfectly moulded, sensuous-looking lips—were quirking, as if he'd got her measure, and that was the last thing she wanted him to have. The man was already weighed down with enough advantages.

'He didn't tell me he was seeing anyone special.' He was leaning back against his desk, his eyes glimmering with suddenly interested speculation.

'Why should he when you don't even return his phone

calls?' The accusation was out before she could check it and once again Emma had cause to regret her impulsive nature. Especially when Piers threw back his head and laughed as though it was the best joke he'd heard in ages.

'Poor hard-done-by Lawrence. Is that the tack you're going to employ? OK, then, let's cut to the chase. I take it you've come to petition me for some money on his behalf?'

'No, of course not! I mean—I mean, I just wanted to talk to you about all the sacrifices he's made lately to finance his new career. To—to demonstrate to you that he's finally found the thing that inspires him most. He told me you always put him down. Won't even give him a chance. Everybody deserves a chance, Mr Redfield. Didn't somebody help you at the start of your famous career?'

Hard work, resilience and the ability to make tough decisions without wavering had taken him to the top, Piers mused passionately. Not a leg up from his father. Now, as he considered the rather arresting brunette in front of him, with her pouty coral lips, honey-brown eyes and the cute little beauty spot just above her left cheek, he could only think it typical that she'd been led to believe that he was the storybook hard-hearted father and Lawrence the poor, misunderstood, rejected son. If he'd been in the mood he could have illuminated her misconceptions with a few unpalatable facts about that poor, misunderstood, rejected son, but Piers didn't see the point when her mind was so obviously already made up.

Glancing down at the Rolex encircling his tanned wrist, he briefly noted the time, then looked pointedly at the young woman in front of him.

'You said sacrifices? What ''sacrifices'' has my son made lately to finance his new career that I should know about? And, by the way, you've got precisely three minutes before I have to go and chair a board meeting.'

'Well...' Clearing her throat, Emma wished she had a glass of water to hand. It wasn't easy to articulate her concerns about Lawrence when her mouth felt as dry as sun-bleached bones. Only now it started to hit her how stupidly presumptuous she'd been in waltzing into the building and infiltrating this man's protected enclave as if she had every right. He was Piers Redfield, for goodness' sake! The role model for aspiring corporate geniuses everywhere, according to his son. Head of one of the premier management consultancies in the country, with a worldwide reputation to match. And not only was his business acumen admired by the great and the good, but he was also awesomely attractive, a fact that Emma hadn't really been prepared for. The man had so much class it practically oozed from his pores, she reflected a little resentfully, reluctantly admiring the beautiful cut of his tasteful dark grey pinstripe suit.

'He sold his car and his motorbike to raise some capital, and they were both his pride and joy, but it's still not enough for him to start up in Cornwall. He'll also need to pay rent on a place as well as buy food. It's going to take a while before the business takes off, but you mark my words, Mr Redfield, it will! Have you any idea how talented your son is?'

'I know exactly what kind of talents my son is endowed with, Miss...?'

'Robards.'

'Miss Robards. But somehow I don't think they're the same ones that you're so keen to endorse. And, for what it's worth, setting up a pottery in an already overcrowded market in the middle of St Ives is not my idea of a viable venture. If you want my opinion, and I'm sure you don't…' The piercing blue eyes frosted over as they swept over her flushed features, causing Emma to bite apprehensively down on her lip. '…it's just another excuse for Lawrence to swan around abdicating all responsibility for his own welfare at my expense. I've given him money more times than I care to mention to finance any number of madcap schemes, and he squandered his mother's legacy in less than a year. I'm afraid as far as I'm concerned he's more than had his quota of help from me. Shame you had a wasted journey, Miss Robards.' And with that Piers walked around his desk and picked up the phone.

Emma could hardly believe he was dismissing her so easily, so coldly, and without consideration. It was his son she'd come to talk about, not some stranger who wasn't anything to do with him! She'd never had a man cry in her arms before, but last night Lawrence had. He'd broken down and poured out all his heartbreak—his lonely, unloved childhood, the death of his poor unhappy mother, driven to numerous affairs during her marriage to Piers because of his addiction to work and making money, and his father's coldness to him whenever he asked for his help. No wonder he hadn't got into university, he'd told her with wounded eyes. No wonder he'd drifted ever since. He was a lost soul and Emma was only too glad to help him in whatever way she could. She might have started out as just the girl who occupied the flat downstairs, but they'd quickly become friends and she'd often fed him when he'd run out of money for food and his cupboards were bare. The least his cold, imperious father could do was hear her out on his behalf!

'Mr Redfield.' Piers glanced up in surprise as Emma crossed the room to the edge of his desk and laid her hand across his where it rested on the receiver. Her skin was exquisitely soft, like the dewy petals of a rose, and he had to curb his surprise at the effect it had on him. A sensual little charge of electricity ran up his arm at her touch and created a nicely warm heat haze in his groin. Time seemed to stand still as all Piers's senses were drowned in the sheer eroticism of the moment. Then, giving himself a mental shake, he moved his gaze to her face and was gratified to see her blush, amused when she quickly withdrew her hand as if he might have something contagious. Was she for real? That becoming colour flooding her cheeks certainly couldn't be faked. He might not admire Lawrence for much, but he could certainly admire his taste in this particular woman. She was too young, of course—twenty-three or -four at most—but she had gumption: that much was clear, or else she wouldn't have risked arriving unannounced in his office to plead her case for his good-for-nothing son. And the way that cerise jacket fitted across that sexy little black stretch top of hers... Well, those delicious curves could keep a man distracted better than the latest Ferrari out of the showroom. Piers withdrew his hand to his trouser pocket, his nostrils flaring slightly as he breathed in deeply to contain his sudden lust.

'Was there something else, Miss Robards?'

'Don't give up on your son. He already feels rejected by you. He needs your help, not your condemnation. He told me to tell you he absolutely promises that this will be the very last time he asks for your help. Can't you just meet up with him for half an hour and hear him out?'

'And what's in it for you, Miss Robards?'

'What do you mean?' Her softly defined brows drew together as she frowned, and her perfume seemed to envelop Piers enticingly as she blushed again. He absorbed the sensation for a long moment as he watched her, registering its impact deep in his belly, deciding he liked the effect it had on him far too much.

'I mean, how does it benefit you if I help Lawrence? Are you looking for an easy life down in the West Country as well?'

He thought... He thought she was pulling some kind of scam to get hold of his money! Emma blanched at the very idea. There wasn't a dishonest bone in her body, and she'd always gone out of her way to help others less fortunate than herself. And this man...this...this arrogant *despot* was suggesting that the only reason she was helping Lawrence was to somehow secure herself an easy life in Cornwall! Her hand itched to slap that conceited smirk right off his too handsome face, but she'd already risked enough trouble without being hauled off for assault as well. Instead she curled it into a fist by her side and told herself to take a deep breath before retaliating.

'I should have known to expect such a low blow from a man such as you,' she said passionately. 'For your information, Mr Redfield, I only came here because Lawrence asked me and I happen to believe in what he wants to do. Personally I'm totally unimpressed by your wealth and wouldn't ask you for a penny if my life depended on it, but Lawrence is a different matter. We're not all cut out to run multimillion-pound corporations, you know. Some of us are struggling with deeper issues that sometimes make it hard for us to find our feet.'

What deeper issues was she struggling with? Piers mused fleetingly before dismissing the thought as irrelevant.

'Are you sleeping with him?'

'What?' Emma stared at him as if he'd just accused her of embezzling all the corporation's funds.

'Let me make it clearer.' Folding his arms across an

impressively wide chest clad in an expensive suit with no doubt impeccable credentials, Piers let his gaze linger for a moment on the fulsome shape of her breasts, lovingly outlined by the black clingy top beneath her jacket. The coming board meeting really wasn't the most pressing thing on his mind right now. 'Are you having sex with my son?'

'How dare you? That's none of your damn business!' Emma was hardly going to tell him that Lawrence had tried to lure her into bed several times since they'd met but, although she was attracted to him, she wasn't ready to make that particular leap of faith just yet. For now she was just happy to think of him as a very good friend.

Besides…he had enough girls parading in and out of his flat, as far as she could see. Like father, like son? According to Lawrence, Piers's love of beautiful women had earned him a reputation as a bit of a playboy. Very aware of that fact, Emma wished her heart wouldn't beat so wildly when he narrowed his penetrating gaze at her as if he was imagining what she looked like without her clothes.

'You must be. Why else would you be championing his cause? Don't be so gullible, Miss Robards. He's only using you, you know. And you wouldn't be the first misguided fool to fall for his dubious charm either.' Sighing, Piers rubbed at his forehead as if a headache had started and Emma was the cause. Then, before she could retaliate, he smiled a slow, knowing little smile that caused a shocking wave of heat to pulsate throughout Emma's body as if she'd suddenly been locked inside a steam room. 'Are you my reward for meeting my son's demands?'

'*What?*' For a crazy instant, Emma told herself she'd imagined the innuendo in his question. She simply couldn't believe that a rich, powerful individual like Piers

Redfield would deign to make a pass at an ordinary girl like her. But then as reality set in, so did anger. Waves of it. 'I can't believe you're insinuating such a foul thing! Lawrence told me your opinion of him was low, but how low I didn't begin to guess. How dare you suggest for even a second that your own son would do such a thing? And even worse—that I...that I would comply with it!'

Piers's glance was unflinchingly direct. 'Then you clearly do not know Lawrence as well as you think you do, Miss Robards. As I said before, he's probably only using you. The sooner you realise it, the better.'

'He's not using me!' she insisted. 'We're good friends. I'd trust Lawrence with my life!'

'Oh, really?' Piers's tone was deliberately scathing. 'Then don't put such a cheap price on it, is my advice to you.'

Emma's slender shoulders sagged dejectedly. It had been a complete waste of time coming to see him. He clearly had no intention and, more to the point, no interest whatsoever in helping his only son. She only hoped he wouldn't have cause to regret it if Lawrence went and did something rash. Was Piers aware that his offspring suffered with chronic depression? Well, now wasn't the time to illuminate him. He looked eager for her to be gone so he could go and chair his obviously far more important board meeting, and frankly Emma didn't feel like subjugating herself to any more far too intimate questions about her love life...or lack of it.

'Whether I'm sleeping with Lawrence or not is neither here nor there,' she said shakily, brown eyes hurt and disappointed. 'All I came here for was to ask you to talk to him, to maybe give him some help...not just financial help, either. He gets very low sometimes and I worry about him. He's not strong like you.' She flushed when Piers's glance became even more piercing.

He was well aware that his son had a deeply melancholic side. But part of Piers still wrestled with the fact that even when things were good for Lawrence, he still managed to muck things up big time. He'd been a greedy and demanding boy who'd only ever thought of himself, and had replicated those less than admirable qualities as an adult, acting as if the world—or at least his father—owed him a living. Piers couldn't even remember how many interviews and meetings he'd set up with friends and clients in business to help Lawrence get his foot in the door. But time and time again he either hadn't shown up for the interview or, if he'd taken the job, had got bored within a week or two and found some pathetic excuse as to why it wasn't exactly what he was looking for. Piers didn't think Lawrence would know what it was he was looking for if it came up behind him and sunk its teeth into his backside. What on earth Emma Robards found remotely appealing about him, apart from his looks, his father could only wonder. Unless, of course, she was hoping that some of Piers's own wealth might trickle down to him.

'Lawrence will survive, mark my words. He's too selfish to do anything that might deprive the world of his presence, so please stop worrying on that score.'

'And that's all you've got to say on the subject?' An ache started between Emma's shoulder blades where anger and disappointment turned her spine into a steel rod instead of cartilage and bone, and she couldn't help but wish that her interview with Lawrence's harsh, uncaring father had not concluded with such a discouraging outcome. Poor Lawrence would be devastated. He'd told Emma before she left that Piers was his last and final hope. The banks just didn't want to know. He had debts outstanding on two big loans already and even his father's illustrious name had not been enough to persuade them to extend him more largesse.

Abruptly bringing the interview to an end, Piers strode to the door and pointedly held it open. Her cheeks burning with embarrassment, Emma walked towards him, her brown eyes desperately trying to conceal the fact that she was close to tears. She hated letting anybody down... especially a friend. When she'd agreed to do as Lawrence asked, she'd taken on the task with such high hopes, even knowing that his father's reputation was formidable. But she could get along with most people, she told herself, and at the end of the day Piers Redfield was only human, wasn't he? And Lawrence was his son...his *only* son.

'Don't take it personally, Miss Robards. It's certainly no failing on your part. You're not responsible for fixing Lawrence's life, and neither am I. He's an adult. He's made his choices and I'm afraid he'll just have to learn to live with them.'

There was not the slightest flicker of regret in those coldly crystalline eyes, Emma noticed indignantly. Not even the smallest notion that another human being might dare question his judgement—his particular choices. Number one being the apparently total abandonment of his only son in his time of need.

'I don't suppose there's anything I can say that would change your mind?' As she raised her hopeful gaze to his, Piers could do nothing about the flash of heat that suddenly throbbed through him. It was not dissimilar to the drenching, languid heat that assailed his body when he was lying out on his terrace in Marbella, but it didn't make him think longingly of margaritas by the pool. No, it conjured up

longings of a very different kind. She had the most bewitching eyes, Piers realised—beautifully framed by the
most lavish dark lashes the colour of warm melted cara-
mel.

'That kind of question could get you into all kinds of
trouble, Miss Robards,' he drawled softly.

Reacting as though he'd just slapped her face, Emma
stood rigid with shock as she stared into his eyes, suddenly
consumed by a sea of such blazing sensuality that every
inch of flesh on her body felt as if it was bathed in warm,
silken honey. Her nipples grew almost painfully tight beneath her shirt and she had to bite back a gasp.

'I—I...' She tried to speak but to her humiliation
couldn't get the words past her throat.

'Take my card.' His voice lowered to a more sensual
cadence, Piers retrieved a business card from his inside
jacket pocket. He pressed it into her hand, briefly and devastatingly curling his fingers around hers. 'Why don't you
give me a ring some time?'

Willing herself to move, Emma tore her gaze away from
his, knowing that if she didn't get out of there soon she
was going to end up in all kinds of trouble. This wasn't
how she had planned it at all! How had she ended up with
Lawrence's high-powered father telling *her* to give him a
ring some time instead of agreeing to a meeting with his
son?

'I have a relationship with your son, Mr Redfield—that's
why I'm here. Doesn't that mean anything to you?
Presumably you're not asking me to ring you to help arrange a meeting with Lawrence?'

Not flinching for a second from her indignant censure,
Piers clenched his jaw, completely unperturbed by the
shock in her eyes. 'What do *you* think, Miss Robards?'

'What do I think? I think you don't deserve to be a

father, that's what I think!' Angrily hefting her briefcase under her arm, Emma tore the little embossed card he'd given her straight down the middle and let the pieces flutter uncaringly to the floor. Disconcertingly, Piers merely smiled enigmatically, his cheekbones deep golden slashes in a face so extraordinarily handsome that once imprinted on a woman's memory it wouldn't be forgotten or relinquished easily.

Shrugging off the insult as easily as brushing a piece of lint off his suit, Piers lifted one corner of his disturbingly attractive mouth in a sardonic little smile. 'Well...if you change your mind, you know where I am.'

Emma turned and fled down the corridor before she said or did something she might definitely have cause to regret.

Returning to his desk, Piers flipped open his diary, glancing down at it unseeingly. There was now no doubt in his mind that Lawrence had deliberately sent the beguiling Emma Robards to do his dirty work for him, and for a moment rage swirled in his gut and clamped his vitals in a vice. Was there no road his feckless son would fail to go down in a bid to get what he wanted? Cursing beneath his breath, Piers dropped down into the black leather chair and deliberately loosened his tie, which just then felt as if it was strangling him. Things between himself and Lawrence just seemed to go from dire to disastrous and right now Piers couldn't think of one damn thing he could do to improve relations. Been there, tried that, been let down more times than any law-abiding parent deserved, in his opinion.

So Lawrence had thought to sweeten his father's attitude towards him by presenting him with a bribe? Did he really believe that Piers wouldn't take him up on it? Maybe he thought his father was too old to be attractive to a pretty young thing like Emma. At the memory of those innocent brown eyes staring back so fetchingly into his, Piers felt inevitable erotic heat settle in his groin. Lawrence should know by now that when it came to a challenge—whether business or personal—Piers was not a man to trifle with.

CHAPTER TWO

'So, HOW did it go with the old man?' His expression wary, blond hair tousled, chest bare and his jeans hung low on his youthful hips, Lawrence strolled into Emma's living-room and dropped down onto the sofa. As he leant forward, his blue eyes were very intense as they flicked across Emma's face. For a moment she didn't know what to say. How was she going to tell him she had failed to get the help he needed when his gaze was so trusting and hopeful? It would be like kicking a dog when he was already down.

'I take it you did get in to see him?' His smile a little nervous, Lawrence helped himself to an apple from the cut-glass bowl on the coffee-table and took a bite. Momentarily surprised by his assumption that she'd actually got that far at least, Emma frowned as she looked at him. 'Don't you believe in wearing clothes? It's November, not the middle of July!'

'I'm OK.' He shrugged his wide shoulders uncaringly. 'I just had a shower. As soon as I heard you come back I just left everything and came downstairs.'

Hearing footsteps walk across the floor above, Emma swallowed down the unexpected hurt that suddenly cramped her throat as she glanced knowingly up at the ceiling. 'Have you got a girl up there?'

For a moment the brilliant blue eyes clouded over. Throwing the half-eaten apple back into the bowl, Lawrence got to his feet and came to join her. 'She means nothing, Em. You know how I've been lately. I just needed

some comfort. Someone to hold.' The unspoken censure
was there in his eyes, Emma realised. He'd had to resort
to someone who 'meant nothing' because Emma refused
to go to bed with him. He slid his hands onto her shoulders, regret and concern competing for her understanding
in his gaze.

Emma swallowed down her disappointment and hurt
and tried to rally her spirits, despite feeling like an ant that
had just been stamped on by an elephant. 'I have feelings
too, Lawrence. I tried to explain to you that I needed more
time. You tell me you want us to be closer, yet you go to
bed with someone else at the first opportunity? I really
don't understand.'

'I'm sorry I hurt you, angel. Please, don't be angry with
me. I know it's hard for you to understand but a man has
needs. You must realise I wouldn't be interested in any
other girl at all if you would just allow yourself to be a
little more intimate with me.'

Telling herself she was too damn forgiving for her own
good, Emma wished she didn't suddenly feel like cry-
ing…and she still hadn't managed to give Lawrence the
bad news yet. 'Anyway, I did manage to see your father.'

'I knew you would.' His hand moved up from her shoulder to settle briefly at the side of her cheek. 'So…how did
it go?'

'Not good, I'm afraid.'

'Oh?' Moving away from Emma, Lawrence strode back
across the room to the sofa and stood in front of it with
his arms folded across his bare chest.

'I'm afraid he won't help.' Hating the fact she was
forced to state things so baldly, Emma chewed down anxiously on her lip, fielding the hurt she already saw reflected
in the dazzling blue irises and wishing there was some way
she could eradicate it forever.

'You explained everything to him? That I wanted to make a new start down in Cornwall? That I wouldn't bother him again if he helps me out just this one last time?'

'Lawrence, I did my best, I really did, but he was resolute. Nothing I said seemed to reach him.'

'Then you clearly didn't try hard enough!' His lips twisting in a scowl, Lawrence glared at Emma as if she were solely responsible for the predicament he found himself in. As his words scorched into her brain, Emma stared back at him, feeling as if she'd just received a sudden, unexpected blow to the head.

'What did you say?' Nervously, she wove her hand through her shoulder-length hair then pulled it free again.

'You know how desperate I am!'

That was it, Emma told herself soothingly. He was only angry with her because he felt so desperate. When he calmed down, everything would be right again between them. But beneath her own assurance another feeling was rising, one that resembled something very close to resentment. Many of her friends—and she herself—had come from far more difficult situations and not everyone had had the cushion of comfort to fall back on that Lawrence had had. Was he right to always expect his father to bail him out of trouble? When did the boy become an adult and start to look after himself?

Glancing at the tall, blond, handsome youth who graced her living-room, Emma experienced a sudden surge of shame that she was silently giving vent to some not so nice feelings about him. It was the ordeal she'd been through, she told herself. It was having Piers Redfield look at her as if he wanted to manoeuvre her up against a wall and take her there and then in his office, with the Lord Mayor's procession weaving through the streets and his staff hanging out of the windows to watch it. Her body throbbed with shameful heat at the thought.

'I'm really sorry that your father won't help but maybe there's another way? Between us we must be able to come up with something.' Forever hopeful, Emma tried to smile consolingly but she could hardly bring herself to look Lawrence in the eye with the thoughts that were currently scorching her brain. Some friend she was.

'Bastard!' Without a thought for Emma's furniture, Lawrence kicked the leg of the coffee-table and sent the glass bowl containing the fruit skidding along its polished surface.

'Lawrence!'

'I suppose he gave you a lecture on how irresponsible and selfish I was? How I don't deserve help because I'm such a dismal failure? Then I suppose he told you how many jobs he'd got me interviews for, how many I didn't turn up to or left after a few days? How I'm always coming up with crazy schemes that go nowhere instead of knuckling down to some ''honest hard work''?'

'He didn't run you down to me.' Distressed by his anger, Emma crossed the room to go to him but he shrugged her off when she reached out to comfort him and glared at her instead.

'What's the matter with you?' His eyes wild, he shook his head. 'You're supposed to be my friend. You know how desperate I've been. You may not mind living in this dump but I *do* mind! I'd do anything to get out of it...anything! Why couldn't you have persuaded him to help me?'

'Persuaded him?' Her dark eyes huge, Emma stared back at Lawrence in stunned disbelief. 'What do you mean, persuaded him?'

'You're a pretty girl, nice breasts, long legs, soft

voice... It can't have been beyond you to try and convince him, can it?'

She felt sick. The room seemed to lurch crazily as all her blood rushed to her head, and she remembered Piers asking her, 'Are you my reward?' Had he guessed right? Had Lawrence expected her to get intimate with his father so that he would help him out? Could her so-called friend really be that ruthless? The thought was so stunningly outrageous that Emma could hardly find words to express her disgust. 'Get out,' she said, her teeth gritted.

'Yeah, well.' Pushing his fingers defiantly through his dishevelled blond hair, Lawrence appeared unaffected by her distress. 'I worry about you, you know, Emma? It's unnatural not to be interested in sex. The only reason Vicky or Nicky, or whatever her name is, is upstairs in my bed is because you're so damned frigid! Either that or you're a lesbian and you haven't told me.'

'I think you've said quite enough for one day.' Her back stiff, Emma walked to the already opened door and held it wide. Biting her lip to stop it from quivering, she watched, chilled, as Lawrence swept past her without another word then pounded up the linoleum-covered stairs to his flat. When he'd gone, she quietly closed her door and leaned back against it with her eyes shut tight.

'You wouldn't be the first misguided fool to fall for his dubious charm,' his father had said, and at the time Emma had believed him to be judging his son completely unfairly. But this was the first time she'd really let him down, she realised. Usually when Lawrence asked a favour of her, she endeavoured to deliver it. Disappointment in her failure to come up with the goods this time must have soured his supposed affection for her—so much so that he couldn't even pretend to be civil. Now she was left with the knowledge that at least his equally ruthless father had been expressing an honest belief when he'd suggested that Lawrence had sent Emma to use her charms to persuade him to cough up financially.

Her stomach churning, Emma pushed away from the door and glanced disconsolately at the clock on the mantel. She had just a couple of hours before she had to be at work and right now she needed a shower to scrub away the taint of the day, though she seriously doubted if she'd ever be able to forget the humiliating events of today. The way she was feeling it would be very easy to blame herself for being such a disappointment to both Redfields. She wasn't sophisticated or clever enough to command genuine regard the way some more worldly women could and consequently she'd allowed both men to treat her with disrespect. Though she wasn't entirely sure that gazing at someone as if they urgently needed to be alone with you in the most intimate way could really be construed as demonstrating disrespect... Remembering the almost overwhelming pull of attraction she had shockingly experienced when she'd looked back into Piers Redfield's disturbingly blue gaze, Emma felt herself grow hot with shame. She had no business lusting after Lawrence's father—however attractive or compelling he might be—and the sooner she put him out of her mind and got back to reality, the better.

Piers had dinner at his club, enjoyed a glass of his favourite French cognac with an old business associate, then got Miles, his driver, to take him home. But once home in the large five-bedroomed Victorian house on the outskirts of Hampstead Heath, he prowled the huge drawing-room then the impressively stocked library with little enthusiasm or interest, a restlessness in his blood that he could neither restrain nor deny. His mind all but drove him crazy with the memory of Emma Robards telling him that he didn't deserve to be a father because he wouldn't help Lawrence and had made a pass at her instead.

Her comment had touched him in a very raw place—an old wound made up of guilt and regret. He'd carefully erected layers of skin as tough as steel around it to stop it from hurting him. But as he recalled it now, it did hurt him. Lawrence might have made a hash of his life so far in terms of getting his act together, but was that really so deserving of Piers's contempt? Was it the boy's fault that his mother had tried to make up for the lack of his father's input by spoiling him rotten and endeavouring to meet every whim and want with meticulous regularity to make up for Piers's absence? Thereby creating an individual just about as selfish as he could be.

'And was it my fault that I was away from home too much because I was trying to build a firm foundation for my family's future? Did Naomi really believe I just did it all for myself?' Piers stalked the floor of the library, his hands alternately deep in his pockets and raking frustratedly through his hair. Emma Robards had opened a can of worms, that was what she'd done. Who the hell did she think she was, stealing into his office uninvited, practically demanding that he finance Lawrence's latest crazy business venture just because they were related by blood?

Recalling those bewitching honey-brown eyes of hers with no difficulty at all, along with the unexpectedly sensual touch of her skin when she had laid her hand across his, Piers silently conceded that he was both intrigued and more than a little attracted to his son's girlfriend. Emma Robards had the kind of chutzpah he admired but she was surely on a lost cause if she was hoping to win Lawrence's undying gratitude for what she'd dared. Piers knew his own son and it didn't take much imagination to work out that when Emma had returned home empty-handed—with no promise of his help, either financial or otherwise—gratitude would be the last thing on Lawrence's mind. He was like a child who'd received every Christmas present he'd ever dreamed of, but still expected there to be one more. No, if Piers wasn't mistaken, the daring Miss Robards would have received nothing more than the raw edge of his son's tongue for her troubles. He almost felt sorry for her. What was she doing with a loser like Lawrence anyway?

Piers swore harshly beneath his breath. It had become all too easy to berate his own flesh and blood. Still, he probably deserved it. Especially after this last little stunt, sending his girlfriend to do his dirty work. Well, this time Piers would pay him back and make him think twice about resorting to such a stunt again. He would help him one last time, he concluded, but in return he wouldn't hesitate to seduce Emma Robards. He'd show his irresponsible son that when it came to matters of strategy, he'd better sharpen his game if he wanted to play with the big boys. As he warmed to the idea, he drove his hand impatiently through his hair one last time then stalked determinedly from the room. In the stunning entrance hall with its black and white tiles and crystal chandelier suspended from the high ceiling, Piers grabbed up his coat from the hall-stand and went out into the cold, rainy night to hail a cab.

'Sorry, Liz. I don't know what's the matter with me this evening.' As Emma stooped to pick up the pieces of broken glass from the kitchen floor, Liz Morrison—friend and co-owner with her husband, Adam, of the bistro known as The Avenue—dropped down to help her. Her smooth forehead wrinkled with concern when she noticed that the younger woman's hands were trembling.

'What's wrong, my love? Has someone upset you?

Those lads are a bit rowdy out there tonight but they're celebrating a friend's promotion. Did one of them say something to you?'

'No, it wasn't them. I'm just feeling a little on edge, that's all. Don't worry.' Getting to her feet, Emma briskly deposited the broken glass into a nearby bin. 'It'll pass.'

'Want to go home early? I can get Louise to stay a bit later to help out.'

'Thanks, but I'll be fine. Really.'

But even as she automatically recited the words, Emma knew she was nowhere near fine. Not after that horrible incident with Lawrence this evening, and the earlier more embarrassing one with his father. It hurt when illusions were destroyed and tonight she'd discovered that Lawrence Redfield wasn't the friend that she'd thought him to be. He'd clearly only used her friendship to advance his own ends, and now all Emma wanted to do was curl up into a tight little ball and make the world go away for a very long time until she felt right again. Only she couldn't do that. She had a life and a job to do, and Liz Morrison had been too good to her for Emma to let her down just because her feelings had been hurt. Smoothing down her neat black skirt then adjusting the matching velvet ribbon on her pony-tail, Emma forced a smile, picked up a tray of glasses to take out to the bar, and headed for the double doors that led into the restaurant.

Liz's hand on her wrist took her by surprise.

'You need a break. Everyone else has taken holidays except you. You haven't even marked out dates on the calendar. I don't flatter myself that work here is so compelling you can't tear yourself away, so what's up, Emma? You can talk to me, can't you?'

Liz Morrison was like a surrogate mother as well as a friend. Her daughter, Fleur, had gone to school with

Emma, and when Fleur departed to Paris to start her career as a very junior dress designer in one of the big fashion houses, Emma had become even more like a second daughter to Liz and Adam. Looking into her concerned, attractive face now, Emma lifted her shoulders and dropped them again.

'I made a fool of myself, Liz, that's all. I'll get over it. And as far as holidays go—well, I just haven't sorted anything out yet.' Only that wasn't strictly true either, Emma thought disconsolately. The plain fact of the matter was that she wasn't in a financial position to take a break. Although she got paid holidays, Emma relied heavily on tips to boost her income, and with her grandmother's operation coming up and all the improvements that needed to be made to her house if she was to return home there afterwards, she needed as much money as she could get. The local authority would only give her a grant for some very basic improvements—the rest, family were supposed to supply. And, as Emma was the only family Helen Robards now had contact with, the responsibility fell to her. Not that Emma minded—far from it. Her grandmother was the one person in all the world who loved her unconditionally and Emma would do anything in her power to bring a little more ease to her life.

'Well, you need to make taking a holiday a priority. Even if all you do is stay at home and potter. You're looking tired. You spend most of your time out of work caring for your gran. I know she's been seriously ill but it isn't right that you should be totally responsible for her care. I'm not a fool, Emma. I know she needs a lot of care and that it's draining you, both physically and financially.'

It was impossible to prevent the wave of self-conscious heat that flooded her cheeks at Liz's perceptive comment. She *did* feel drained. But what could she do about it when there was no one else to share the burden of her grand-mother's care?

'I won't pretend it's not tough sometimes but she's my only family, Liz. Yes, I'd love a holiday but right now it's not an option. Not even remotely.'

Liz smiled in understanding. 'I'm not getting on to you, Emma, love. I'm just concerned. Still worried about Gran's operation?'

Emma nodded, yet couldn't help smiling at the thought of her grandmother's determination to get better. 'She's tough though, you know? She'll be OK. And if it makes you feel any better I'll book some time off in a fortnight. That's a week before the op, and I can be with Gran and keep an eye on her before she goes into hospital.'

'Well, if either of you needs anything—anything at all—you must let me know. Promise?'

'Promise. But you're too good to me, you know that?'

'Someone's got to look out for you, love. Now, you'd better go and help Lorenzo in the bar or he'll be in here screaming for those glasses any second now!'

An hour later, Emma glanced up from stacking glasses behind the bar and froze. Staring back at her from the doorway where he had just come in from the cold, Piers Redfield's burning blue gaze closed the distance between them as though they stood head to head. She almost dropped another glass in her bid to extricate herself from the intensity of his examination, glancing helplessly at the handsome Lorenzo as he stood by her side humming along to the music that was playing softly, but unable to find words to elucidate her distress. What on earth was he doing here? Had Lawrence sent him? Had Piers decided to press charges or something equally horrendous because Emma had had the audacity to inveigle her way into his private office?

Finally realising they had another customer and before Emma could find her voice, Lorenzo dashed out from behind the bar to greet the imposing-looking man in the damp trenchcoat, speaking to him enthusiastically in his drawling Italian accent as Emma looked on, aghast. Then, shaking Piers's hand and taking his coat, he led him to a secluded table for two in one of the dimly lit recesses with their dark oak seating. He laughed at something Piers said as he bent his head briefly to light the lone white candle in the centre of the table. Emma's stomach knotted with deep foreboding. She noted a couple of women at one of the nearby tables glance across the almost full restaurant at Piers. Bending their heads, they whispered something and giggled. It didn't take a genius to guess what had just passed between them. Piers was easily the most attractive and dynamic-looking man in the room, and Emma didn't suppose there were too many crowded restaurants where that wouldn't be the case.

Taking a deep lungful of air, she busied herself with drying glasses until Lorenzo hung up Piers's coat then returned to the bar.

'Emma, can you take the man in the corner a menu, please?'

It wasn't like her to be so slow on the uptake but then it wasn't every night she had a good reason to hang back. Her nervous brown eyes glanced helplessly into Lorenzo's deep black. 'Can't you do it? I'm—I'm busy with these glasses.'

The young Italian restaurant manager shook his head in clear disapproval. 'First you break all my glasses then you refuse to serve a customer. What is wrong with you this evening, Emma?'

A fierce blush coloured her otherwise pale cheeks. 'I'm

not refusing to serve anybody, I'm just busy doing something else.'

Without a word, Lorenzo reached for something on the corner of the bar and dropped a leather-bound menu into her hands. 'Enough of this nonsense! Take the man a menu and for the love of God look happy about it!'

Now she knew how those French aristocrats must have felt on their way to the guillotine. Her legs almost buckling beneath her, Emma took her time negotiating her way past tables, a smile fixed on her face that felt more like a mask. When she reached Piers's table, she held out the menu and lost the smile altogether.

'What are you doing here?' she asked, her voice barely above a strangled whisper. Completely unfazed, Piers took the menu without a word and opened it. Pretending interest, he idly flipped through the beautifully bound pages and smiled. It was the smile of a big cat that had just cornered his prey and was now toying with it before the inevitable took place.

'I heard this was a good place to eat. What would you recommend this evening?'

'You haven't really come here to eat at all, have you?' Her anxious glance suddenly trapped by his remarkable blue eyes, Emma's stomach clenched painfully. Soundlessly closing the menu then placing it carefully down on the table, Piers linked his hands together and considered her with all the serious deliberation of a judge about to pronounce sentence.

'Astute as well as daring. You're a constant surprise, Miss Robards.'

'What's this all about? Why have you come here? Did Lawrence send you?'

'Now, why would he do that?'

To punish me…to make me suffer because I didn't get

him what he wanted… Emma put her hand to her mouth to stop herself from pleading with him to go away and leave her alone. Already Lorenzo was looking over at her from the bar, a suspicious frown between his smooth black brows. 'I don't know. Why would a Redfield do anything?'

'Is that an insult I hear in your voice, Emma? You don't mind if I call you Emma?'

'Please.' Nervously running her hand across her hair, she leant closer, her words intended for his ears only. 'If you're angry with me for coming to see you on Lawrence's behalf, I'm very sorry. If you want to know the truth, I regret every second and I swear to you it will never happen again. Now, will you please go before my manager gets even more suspicious?'

'You're right. I didn't come here to eat.' Before she realised his intention, Piers had snagged her hand and held it, a glimmer in the seductive depths of those deeply crystalline blue eyes that sent Emma's heart racing in a futile search for somewhere to hide. His touch made her hot all over and the faint musky tang of his aftershave enveloped her in a sudden paroxysm of fear and anticipation. 'I went to see Lawrence. He told me you worked here. You and I have to talk.'

'Why did he tell you where I work? What do you want from me, Mr Redfield? Please tell me quickly so that I can get back to work.' She snatched her hand away and rubbed it as if to erase his touch.

Piers frowned. He wasn't used to women responding to him in such a negative way and, frankly, it irked him. Did she still nurse hopes for herself and Lawrence? Was that the way of it? If so, she was on a hiding to nothing because when Lawrence had answered the door to him earlier, his errant son had clearly had company. Company of the bedroom kind—a cute little blonde with an impish smile and breasts to write eulogies to if that tight red dress she'd been wearing was any true indication of the facts. After he'd agreed to furnish Lawrence with twice the amount he needed to set up in Cornwall, his son would have told Piers anything he cared to know. It had been easy to get him to reveal the name and location of the bistro where his pretty neighbour worked. Lawrence himself had mentioned it during the course of their conversation—no doubt to lessen Emma's appeal by revealing that she was a waitress and not in a league his father would be interested in. 'Why would a Redfield do anything?' Emma had suspiciously asked… Why indeed? Perhaps ruthlessness ran in the blood after all?

Now, as he sat staring up at the beautiful girl his son had thought to use to further his own ends, Piers felt that same blood in his veins heat and slow with all the excitement and anticipation of fierce desire. All the aces were on his side if he played his cards right, and if she was sweet to him Piers would reward her with anything her little heart desired…

'What time do you finish?'

Emma reluctantly told him.

'I'll wait and take you home. It'll have to be a cab; my driver's gone home for the night.'

'Your driver?'

'Chauffeur, then. Anyway, as I said, I'll wait and take you home, then we can talk.'

'No!'

'No?'

'I mean, I don't want you to wait and take me home and I definitely don't want to talk to you, Mr Redfield! What can you possibly have to say to me that would be of interest? I've already apologised for sneaking into your office; what more do you want?'

His blue eyes went so dark that Emma stepped back from the table as though a hot lick of flame had suddenly scorched her tender skin. Her blush was so deep she felt sure everyone in the room must notice it. In fact Lorenzo was headed her way right this second—no doubt angry that she seemed to be antagonising his customer—because it was plain to see that Piers wasn't smiling.

'Is everything all right?' He specifically addressed Piers, but his suspicious gaze broke away for all of a couple of seconds to silently rebuke Emma.

'Everything is fine. *Grazie.*' To her amazement, Piers started to converse with Lorenzo in what sounded like flawless Italian and the younger man, obviously delighted and surprised, responded enthusiastically in his native tongue as though they were long-lost buddies. Relieved that Lorenzo wasn't about to berate her in front of Piers, Emma moved to make herself scarce, and was shocked when Lorenzo waved her commandingly into the seat opposite Piers and all but pushed her down into it.

'I am cross with you, Emma, that you didn't tell me that this man was your fiancé! Even if you had a fight you must not keep such secrets from me, huh? I am your friend as well as your manager.'

'But he's not my—'

Beneath the table Piers gave her ankle a sharp kick. Glaring at him with pointed little daggers of pure dislike, Emma wondered what the hell he thought he was playing at. Of all the things he could have said, what on earth had possessed him to tell Lorenzo that they were engaged to be married?

CHAPTER THREE

'I WILL bring that bottle of wine *pronto!* Emma, you must take the rest of the evening off. *Scusi,* Mr Redfield, I will be back in a moment.'

When they were alone, Emma struggled for all of two seconds to contain the anger that was threatening to burst like a dam.

'How dare you lie to him? How will I explain to him later that it was just some kind of sick joke? I don't know what you're playing at, Mr Redfield, but whatever it is I don't want any part of it!'

'For your information, *Miss* Robards, I'm not playing. When I see something I want I cut right to the chase—whatever it takes. Do I make myself clear?' His penetrating gaze signalled his seriousness and Emma felt her stomach flip over in fright. Was he saying that he wanted her? What had she done to warrant such unasked-for attention? This man was rich beyond imagining and could clearly have any woman he set his sights on—so why had he set his sights on her? An insignificant little waitress who'd championed his son's cause because he was in need and she'd mistakenly believed he was a true friend.

'It's not clear at all.' Her face burning, Emma fiddled with the little silver napkin ring in front of her. 'I don't know what you want from me.' Finally risking a direct glance, she saw a corner of his mouth hitch up slightly into what could be the beginnings of a smile—only she wasn't entirely sure. Everything about him inspired awe, from the width of those amazing shoulders in his exqui-

37

sitely tailored suit, to the clean-cut edge of his hard, chis-
elled jaw and those scintillating eyes that clearly didn't
miss a trick. Imagining him as chairman of the board at
meetings with the country's most prominent and influential
businessmen and entrepreneurs, Emma knew there'd be a
respectful hush when he entered the room.

'Your attention is what I want, Emma.'

'And you had to tell Lorenzo you were my fiancé to get
it?'

'Whatever it takes, remember? How old are you?' he
asked, amused.

'Twenty-five.' Her guard down, Emma widened her
dark eyes in puzzlement. 'Why do you ask?'

'Because you look more like nineteen. Tell me. Are you
serious about Lawrence?'

The steely muscles that made up the hard wall of his
stomach actually clenched as Piers waited for her to answer. Her features were compellingly beautiful, with skin
as fine and pale as alabaster and eyes and lips a man could
happily gaze at until he grew old—yet she was also possessed of an extraordinary innocence that intrigued Piers
even more. He could hardly believe she didn't know what
kind of effect she could have on a man, but that was the
impression he was getting. Look at him, he thought wryly.
Just one encounter with her and he'd gone against all his
principles and signed Lawrence a cheque for a ridiculous
amount to set up some pie-in-the-sky little venture that was
surely doomed to failure before it even started. He'd have
been better off just throwing his money into an incinerator.

'I don't know what you mean.' Flushing, Emma glanced
up almost with relief as Lorenzo descended upon them,
flourishing a bottle of the best red wine in the house.
Addressing Piers, the young Italian poured the wine, all
the while chattering away in his native tongue, then left

them to, 'Enjoy, enjoy!' with a final departing wink in Emma's direction and a too knowing smile as he slid behind the bar again.

His fingers sliding around the stem of his wineglass, Piers continued to survey her with an unnerving intensity that made it difficult to corral her thoughts. 'Would you be heartbroken if you didn't see him again?'

'Why? Is he going somewhere?'

'Cornwall, if everything goes to plan.' Piers shrugged as if he had his doubts.

'Then you agreed to help him?' Her mouth dropping open, Emma couldn't disguise her astonishment.

'Let's just say I had second thoughts after you left.'

'He must have been over the moon.'

'I left him getting ready to go out and celebrate with his lady friend.'

'Oh.'

'You don't mind?' Watching closely for signs of hurt or distress, Piers was gratified when he found none. Instead she looked resigned.

'Our relationship isn't like that.'

'Sexual, you mean?'

Emma felt the heat in her face deepen. 'Lawrence has lots of girlfriends but our association is purely platonic.'

One fair brow jutted towards his hairline. 'You're telling me you didn't sleep with him?'

Emma sighed and took a careful sip of the dark red wine that Lorenzo had poured out for her. Her tastebuds barely registered the smouldering burst of grape on her tongue. 'Look, where is this leading? I hardly know you and yet you sit there expecting me to discuss my private life with you as though it was the most natural thing in the world. I'm glad you decided to help your son, Mr Redfield, but as far as he and I are concerned, I don't actually care if I never set eyes on him again!'

'So he gave you a hard time when you told him I wasn't going to help?' Raking his fingers through his dark blond hair, Piers sat back in his seat and shook his head. 'That figures.'

'Look, I really should get back to work.'

'Stay right where you are.' Emma suddenly found she had his undivided attention again. Heat ignited in his eyes with all the impact of a dazzling white flare against a coal-black sky, and an answering shiver zigzagged down her spine. 'We're supposed to be engaged, remember? You don't want Lorenzo over there to think we've had another fight, do you?'

'I don't care what he thinks, considering this whole thing is a complete farce!'

'I want to see you again.'

'Why... For what reason?'

'Because you intrigue me. Isn't that reason enough?'

She'd never had a man tell her that she intrigued him before and the fact that Piers Redfield—who was generally regarded as a phenomenon himself—said so was more than a little difficult to take in. Try impossible. Emma could only draw the conclusion that he must be up to something...but what?

'So, you're intrigued by waitresses? With some men it's lap dancers or nurses but obviously you—'

'Emma.'

The soft yet steely command in his voice stopped her dead. Her heart started to race again and she wished her face wouldn't burn so. 'What?'

'I don't have a fetish for waitresses. Though I'd be lying if I said you didn't look extremely sexy in that tight black skirt.'

In fact Piers had never seen another woman look half so good in a tight black skirt. Emma was slender but her figure was definitely hourglass-shaped and her fitted clothes showed just how delectable that shape was. Now she was blushing again and Piers sensed his attraction deepening. Surely she was used to men paying her compliments all the time? But there was nothing coy about her response. She merely looked flustered and uncertain, like a young girl out on her first proper date.

She's too young for you, urged the voice of reason. But Piers was in too deep to pay much attention to it. He was only forty-two, for God's sake! Nowhere near a mid-life crisis or anything as dull as that, and he didn't particularly lust after younger women. He'd dated plenty of women his own age and older. He simply enjoyed the company of beautiful women. In his career he'd met many, but he'd never yet met one who intrigued him enough to make that relationship permanent. As far as he was concerned, marriage was out. Been there, tried that and, apart from a few short months when Lawrence was a baby and he and Naomi had felt like a real family instead of two angry people who merely tolerated each other, Piers had hated it. Freedom was far preferable in his opinion.

'It's not tight, it's fitted, and I'm not pursuing this pointless conversation with you any longer. I've got to get back to work. We're already a girl short tonight and you can see that we're busy.' Getting to her feet, Emma threw Piers a last flustered look and walked away.

'Damn.' Piers's male friends envied the ease at which women seemed to fall over themselves to get to know him, but somehow tonight it seemed his famed ability had vanished. He was left in no doubt that he'd failed to impress or attract Emma Robards. Signalling a passing young waiter, Piers paid his bill, collected his coat and walked back out into the cold, wintry night, not caring that the rain showed no mercy as it pelted him hell for leather as he walked.

'Why did that man tell Lorenzo you and he were engaged if you're not?' Cradling her much-needed cup of coffee, Liz Morrison sat across the cleared table from Emma in the now empty restaurant, endeavouring to get to the bottom of the most surprising thing that had happened all evening.

'Oh, he was just playing stupid games.' Emma shrugged, momentarily shielding her expression behind her own coffee-cup. *I'm not playing,* he'd said, but clearly he'd lied. She really had no idea why he'd taken the trouble to come to the bistro and find her and nor did she buy the reason he had given—that he was somehow 'intrigued' by her. So 'playing stupid games' was all her befuddled brain could come up with.

'He was rather gorgeous all the same. When Lorenzo came into the kitchen and told me I sneaked a look while you weren't looking. Where did you meet him?' Liz asked conversationally. But behind her employer's deceptively casual tone, Emma knew there was a wealth of curiosity just bursting to get out. Liz was always trying to fix Emma up with some suitable male or other but was continually frustrated by the younger woman's inexplicable lack of interest.

'Oh, he's a friend of a friend.' Hoping to brush him off as just that, Emma prayed they could now change the subject. Piers Redfield's name and presence had simply dominated her day too much. It was time to get back to reality. Not always easy, but at least it was a devil she knew.

'Well, I certainly wouldn't kick him out of bed.'

'Liz!' Aghast, Emma stared at the other woman as if she had just confessed to some heinous crime.

'You know very well I love Adam, but it doesn't mean I can't appreciate another man's good looks, does it? And your friend of a friend was certainly worth taking a second look at. Loved the suit too. Bet that cost a pretty penny.'

'I wouldn't know.'

'Oh, for God's sake, Emma! You're a beautiful young woman and you've got about as much interest in the opposite sex as somebody who's gay!' Her hazel eyes suddenly narrowing, Liz lowered her voice conspiratorially. 'You're not gay, are you, darling?'

'No!' Not knowing whether to laugh or cry, Emma put down her coffee-cup and licked the cream from her top lip. 'I can assure you I'm not gay.' It was the second reference to her sexual proclivities that day—first Lawrence's hurtful jibe, now her friend's concerned probe. So what if she didn't have a relationship? Why did everyone seem to believe that coupledom was the only important choice in life? Couldn't they see that most people's relationships fell apart on a regular basis? Who needed the grief? All she had to do was remember how heartbroken her mother had been when Emma's father had walked out on them when Emma was only nine. She'd never really recovered and they'd never set eyes on him again. They'd heard from a friend of his who'd come around to the house once that he'd emigrated to Australia soon after the divorce he'd insisted on, but after that…nothing. He never even kept in touch with his own mother—Emma's beloved Gran. He'd obviously wiped out the memory of his previous life with heartless precision and had disowned them both. So who needed a man? Certainly not Emma—not right now, and probably not ever.

But just as she reaffirmed her decision to remain single

to herself, an uncalled-for recollection of Piers Redfield's crystalline blue eyes sliding hotly down her body brought a flush of warmth to parts of her anatomy that hadn't experienced that sensation in a very long time...

'Men are a hassle. I have enough to deal with without getting screwed up by some relationship. Stop worrying about me, Liz. I'm really quite happy in my single state.'

'So tell me a bit more about the guy who came in earlier.'

Smiling in spite of her exasperation at Liz's tenacity where Piers Redfield was concerned, Emma got up, pushed her chair into the table, and went to collect her coat from the nearby coat tree. 'Trust me. You won't be seeing him again.' If Liz even had an inkling of who he was, she wouldn't let Emma leave the restaurant until she'd told her everything and Emma had had enough embarrassment for one day, thank you very much.

'You and your fiancé had another fight?' Lorenzo shook his head in deep disapproval as he came through the swing doors with his leather jacket on. He being true to his Italian blood, the one thing he held in high esteem was *amore*. 'Emma, Emma! What did you say to make him leave? He didn't even stay to eat!'

'Once and for all, Piers Redfield *isn't* my fiancé!'

As Liz Morrison got to her feet, her surprised glance sprang to the younger woman with all the speed of an arrow hitting the bull's-eye. Her husband read the financial pages of his chosen broadsheet every day and she knew only too well where she'd heard that illustrious name.

'*That* was Piers Redfield?' she yelped. '*The* Piers Redfield?'

Emma's body turned hot then cold. Nonplussed, Lorenzo glanced from one woman to the other and back again. 'Is he famous?'

'Not in the sense that Brad Pitt or Hugh Grant is famous but the guy's on the UK Rich List, that's for sure. Emma, you dark horse! What on earth is going on?'

'Hey, Piers! You were fierce out there today. What's going on?' As his friend and colleague hurried to catch up to him in the locker-room of the exclusive sports club of which they were both members, Piers unzipped his bag, pulled out his towel and draped it around his neck. The sweat he'd expended on the squash court dampened his hair and stood out in beads on his brow but still he hadn't been entirely able to get rid of some of that huge reservoir of energy that had been flowing through him all day. God only knew how he was going to sleep tonight but if the previous five nights were anything to go by, he'd be watching the dawn come up again tomorrow having hardly slept a wink.

'Nothing's going on.' Peeling off his clothes, Piers wrapped a second towel around his lean, hard middle, collected his washbag then disappeared in the direction of the showers across the cool tiled floor.

'Not getting any lately? Is that the trouble, hotshot?' Jim Delaney, an affable American and Piers's regular squash and racketball partner, laughed out loud before disappearing into an adjoining cubicle. As the water built up a head of steam and sluiced down his hot, aching body, Piers couldn't suppress the colourful language that escaped with his next few breaths. Leave it to Jim to stumble across the truth without even knowing it. But it wasn't just the fact he wasn't getting any, as his friend had so crudely put it— it was the fact that he was lusting after a twenty-five-year-old waitress who'd rather work than take the night off and spend it with him. In terms of experiences with women, this had to be a first. Usually it was the women who did all the chasing and, although he was partly ashamed to admit it, Piers had got used to cherry-picking the best. Now, as he glanced down at the manifestation of his sexual frustration, Piers knew that as far as Emma Robards was concerned he would have to come up with something quite unique to get her attention…but get it he would.

Emma couldn't sleep. A mole hibernating for the winter couldn't sleep with that racket going on upstairs. What on earth was Lawrence doing? She'd heard the feminine laughter that accompanied the general noise and mayhem and blushed to think what he might be up to. For a moment the thought had the power to wound but then irritation finally got the better of her and she threw back the bedcovers, shoved her feet into slippers and went through to the kitchen to make a cup of tea. Yawning as she filled the kettle, she glanced around the tiny, cramped kitchen with little pleasure. The pink paint she'd applied to the walls only six months ago in a bid to cheer the place up had already started to crack and peel. Her dark eyes seeking out the culprit, she noted the increasingly large patches of damp on the ceiling and on the walls. She'd been on to the landlord several times already about getting something done about it, but if past experience was anything to go by she'd be waiting for a response until she drew her old-age pension. The flat needed lots of work. More than Emma could afford. She was already fretting about how she was going to find the money to help her grandmother make necessary home improvements, so she hadn't a cat's chance in hell of finding enough cash to do up her own place.

Sighing, she reached up to the hooks on the wall for a cheerful mug with a bright yellow daffodil on it, then threw in a teabag. Lucky old Lawrence, escaping to

Cornwall. Right now she'd jump at the chance. Though of course not with him. They'd hardly exchanged two words since the afternoon he'd accused her of being frigid and possibly a lesbian and, quite frankly, Emma didn't care. At first she thought she'd miss his regular visits and 'putting the world to rights' conversations, but how could she miss someone who wasn't really the person she'd thought him to be in the first place? Lawrence hadn't been a true friend. If he had, he wouldn't have been so nasty to her when she'd told him his father wasn't going to help get him out of the fix he was in. And he most definitely wouldn't have expected her to use her feminine assets to get the result he'd wanted. He would have been grateful that she'd at least tried—at great personal risk too.

But it was all academic now because Piers had decided to help his son after all and so Lawrence was packing up lock, stock and barrel to go down to Cornwall and a new start. *Piers*... When had she begun to address him with such startling familiarity? She'd only met the man twice, for goodness' sake, and neither encounter had been exactly pleasant. Pouring hot water into the waiting mug, Emma bit down guiltily on her lip. That wasn't exactly true, she recalled, remembering the way he had complimented her figure in her 'tight' black skirt. But the man was altogether too sure of himself, too arrogant and too...too rich! What else had he been doing but playing games, seeking her out at the restaurant where she worked? Perhaps he'd had a slow day at the stock exchange and was looking for some kind of diversion? Yeah...as if a man like Piers Redfield had to resort to chasing two-a-penny waitresses to get his kicks these days!

But all the same, the man had got to her. That fact alone scared Emma witless. After an abortive attempt at a relationship shortly after her nineteenth birthday, Emma had more or less decided on the single life. The man she'd been involved with had been an economics lecturer at her secretarial college who'd told her at the time that he was divorced and living alone. Three months into the relationship Emma had found out that he was still married, living quite amicably with his wife and was the father of two young children. His deceit had made her feel used and dirty, and merely confirmed what she'd known all along— that she was better off on her own. She hadn't even wanted to stay and get her diploma. Instead she'd decided on a complete change of pace and, at her friend Fleur's instigation, had gone to work for Liz and Adam Morrison at The Avenue, a popular and trendy bistro not far from where Emma lived.

Six years later she was still there. 'So?' she muttered aloud. 'We're not all cut out to be rocket scientists or corporate millionaires. Some of us have responsibilities.' Giving her tea a vigorous stir, Emma shrugged off more threatening introspection and glared up instead at the ceiling, where several heavy thumps suddenly echoed.

'What the hell are you doing up there, Lawrence?'

Minutes later, her short eau-de-Nil silk wrap that had been a rare extravagance fastened securely at the waist, Emma pounded up the stairs to find out what was going on. It didn't surprise or faze her when Lawrence answered the door wearing nothing but navy blue boxers with a cheerful football motif on and a cheeky grin as wide as the English Channel.

'Emma, my darling! Am I keeping you awake?'

'You know damn well you are!' Peering past his shoulder into the room beyond, Emma stared in disbelief at the mess—in the middle of which sat some kind of wire and clay monstrosity that vaguely resembled a man with his head in his hands. 'What on earth are you doing at this time of night? It sounds as if you're digging your own Channel Tunnel in the living room! Did it ever occur to you that some of us need to sleep?'

'Well…you know Rodin's *Thinker?* Well, it inspired me to come up with something similar. I can't just do pottery, Em, it would drive me stark, staring mad, so I'm diversifying into some sculpture. I've called it, *Now the Thinking's Over.* Cool, huh?'

Emma told herself she was having a bad dream. 'You are as mad as a March hare!'

Lawrence grinned back, unabashed. 'Wasn't it the Hatter who was supposed to be mad?'

'I don't believe I'm having this conversation.' Folding her arms crossly across her chest, Emma scowled. 'It's all very well having an artistic urge in the middle of the night, Lawrence, but surely even you must have realised that other people need to sleep so they can work the next day?'

'I'm sorry, sweetheart, I truly am, but now that you're here there was something I wanted to say to you.' Taking a surreptitious glance over his shoulder, Lawrence stepped out into the draughty passage, flicked up the catch and pulled the door behind him. 'Vicky's the jealous type, I'm afraid. Wouldn't be happy seeing me talking to another woman dressed only in her nightwear…very nice nightwear, too.'

Releasing a long-suffering sigh, Emma rolled her eyes. Face to face with Lawrence for the first time since the unpleasantness between them, she realised very quickly she was anything but heartbroken about him and his latest girlfriend.

'So you've established at least that her name is Vicky, not Nicky?'

'Pardon?'

'Never mind. What was it you wanted to tell me?' Shivering, Emma briskly rubbed her chilled arms beneath the thin silk of her robe.

'I'm really sorry for what I said the other day. It was totally out of order and frankly I didn't expect you to ever want to speak to me again. And I didn't really expect you to persuade my father in the way I hinted. You do believe me, don't you?'

Emma's foolish heart squeezed at the earnestness on his boyish face. She'd always known she was a pushover, and this probably just confirmed it. 'You're forgiven,' she said, shrugging. 'You're starting a new life down in Cornwall… I don't want us to part on bad terms.'

'Thanks, Em. And it's totally down to you that I'm able to go in the first place. If you hadn't gone to the old man on my behalf I would never—'

'He's not old.' Her interruption was automatic.

Lawrence's blue eyes narrowed. 'He's not in bad shape for forty-two, I agree.'

*Forty-two? He looks more like thirty-five…*Emma mused silently, then guiltily caught the flicker of deeper interest that flashed across Lawrence's face. 'He's always been able to turn on the charm with women but I don't suppose being filthy rich hurts either,' he said disparagingly.

Dismayed at his attitude, Emma glanced down at the cracked terracotta linoleum under her feet. 'Anyway, he agreed to help you in the end. He can't be all bad.'

'Taking his side, are you?' There was a flash of temper in the deceptively friendly blue eyes and Emma's stomach roiled a little.

'I'm not taking anyone's side,' she said dismissively. 'Your father's the last person in the world who needs someone to champion him, least of all me.'

'I wish you were coming with me instead of Vicky.'

Reaching out his hand, Lawrence let his finger trail softly down Emma's cheek. 'We could have been good together, Em. You understand me better than anybody else I know.'

Not true, Emma thought sadly. She was only too painfully aware just how badly she'd misjudged her friend's character. Stepping back out of reach, she touched her cheek where he'd trailed his finger, wishing she could erase his touch forever. 'You'll be much better off with Vicky, I'm sure. Besides, I could never have gone with you, Lawrence. Not with my gran just about to go into hospital.'

'She's lucky to have such a kind, caring granddaughter.'

'You'd love her too if you knew her.' Shivering on the draughty landing, Emma smiled briefly then put her hand on the banister to go back downstairs. 'I'm glad your father's decided to help you,' she said, quickly changing the subject. Sometimes just the thought of her gran and the operation she had to face was just too overwhelming. 'When you're settled, perhaps I'll come down and visit.'

'Yes, you must.'

'Well.' Emma smiled and shrugged again, then turned towards the stairs. 'I'll see you around...and Lawrence?'

'Yes, Em?'

'I respect your creative impulses but please could you try keeping the noise down?'

'Sure. Anything for you, angel.' Blowing her a kiss, Lawrence turned and went inside.

CHAPTER FOUR

'EMMA…he's out there!'

'Who?' But even as Liz clutched her by her shirtsleeve, Emma knew exactly who. Some inner sixth sense had made her watch her back from the moment she'd stepped through the door of the bistro around eleven that morning. Now as the two chefs, Paul and Marco, busied themselves around the bustling, hot kitchen, Emma stared at Liz and felt her knees almost buckle beneath her.

'You must have made quite an impression for him to come back this soon. Shame he's with another woman, though.'

Emma told herself to breathe. Now what was he playing at? Whatever it was, it was a game she didn't understand, and didn't want to. All she wanted was for Piers Redfield to get out of her life and stay out. She rued the day she'd agreed to help Lawrence by going to see him.

'Has he ordered food?' she found herself asking. Examining her as if she was a crazy woman, Liz put her hands on her hips and shook her head. 'No. People come into a restaurant at lunchtime to admire the décor… What do you think?'

Sliding her too warm hands down the sides of her skirt, Emma wished her heartbeat would return to normal so that she could think. 'So he's had a menu?'

'No, darling. He specifically asked for you to bring it.' Without further preamble, Liz picked up two leather-bound menus from the trolley behind her and shoved them into Emma's hands.

52

'Take them to him, there's a good girl. And put a smile on your face or you'll frighten the customers!'

Hanging back, Emma chewed down on her lip, her dark eyes huge and anxious as she stared back at Liz. 'Tell him I'm indisposed…or…or tell him I've just had to pop out for a while! Tell him I've gone to the dentist. Please, Liz. Tell him anything you like but don't make me go out there and speak to him. Please!'

'Has he offended you in some way or said something to upset you?'

'Not…specifically, no.'

'Then what's all the fuss about?' Stepping aside as Marco squeezed past them in search of his number-one frying pan, Liz parted her red lips in a reassuring smile. 'He's just a man at the end of the day, sweetie. Granted, he might have more money than you could shake a stick at, but that doesn't mean he doesn't have needs just like anyone else and right now the man needs to eat. So take him the menu, smile that gorgeous smile of yours and keep him happy! You never know—next week he might be back with some of his rich friends. I can't tell you what *that* would do for business!'

So Emma found herself making her way with trepidation past the lunchtime crowd who were rapidly filling the tables to present Piers with a menu. He sat in one of the alcoves again, this time with a very attractive, extremely elegant blonde in a little black dress that looked as if it would cost Emma a year's salary at least. There was a moneyed air around both of them, and already other customers were turning to look, perhaps silently speculating as to who they might be. Gathering up all her courage, Emma managed a smile just one notch up from frozen, presented Piers and his friend with their menus then stood back while his amused blue eyes silently and languidly appraised her.

'Well, if it isn't my favourite waitress.'

She had a ridiculous desire to curtsy just to mock him, but when Piers's gaze slid deliberately down her body in her white silk shirt, fitted black skirt and black hosiery he clearly wasn't contemplating food and Emma's courage almost marched out the door.

'Mr Redfield…what brings you back to us so soon?'

It was a question she hardly expected a reply to but she asked it anyway just to be contentious.

'You have to ask?' he drawled smoothly.

'Piers told me he'd found this quaint little bistro quite off the beaten track,' his blonde companion purred, her perfectly lipsticked smile for him alone. 'It really is quite sweet. I hope the food is good… Is it?'

'The Avenue might be off the beaten track, as you put it, but I can assure you we have a regular and very satisfied clientele because the food is second to none.'

'In that case, what do you recommend?' Piers asked, opening his menu. His cologne drifted under Emma's nostrils and almost scrambled her brain with its latent sexiness. When he stopped studying the menu to give her his full and exclusive attention, Emma shivered, wishing she knew a handy conjuring trick to make herself disappear.

'What do I recommend?' She blinked, like an owl trying to adjust its sight to the dawn. 'Erm…it depends whether you prefer a vegetarian option or…or meat.'

'Got any fish on the menu?'

'Yes.' Her cheeks burning, Emma prayed for the day's selection to helpfully spring to mind. 'We have a very good bouillabaisse that's very popular and also monkfish with Muscadet and cream. And—and all the meals are served with fresh seasonal vegetables or a green salad.'

She felt like an inexperienced junior on her very first day in the restaurant and hated every moment she stood there, while in contrast Piers appeared to find great amusement in her discomfort.

'Caroline? Are you happy to go with the monkfish?'

His companion would happily eat sheep's eyes if Piers thought it was a good idea, Emma observed scornfully.

'We'll go with the monkfish and vegetables, and could you bring us some wine?' He named a specific white that Emma knew straight away was the most exclusive bottle of wine on the menu.

'Of course.' Gathering up the menus, relief at being allowed a reprieve from such rarefied company already making her breathe more easily, Emma flinched in shock when Piers's hand came out and caught hold of hers. 'I'd like to speak to you afterwards... Can you spare five minutes?'

Glancing anxiously at the blonde Caroline, who was busy delving into her purse for something, Emma hardly knew what to say, especially when Piers held on to her hand when she would have tugged it free. 'I—we're very busy. Can it wait until another time?'

'No. It can't.'

The pad of his thumb stroked the soft, delicate skin just below her knuckles, making no secret of the fact. For a moment or two Emma completely lost her bearings. It was apparent he felt her tremble just before she discreetly pulled her hand free—the reaction of his suddenly darkened pupils attested to that and she'd bet her best ever tip that he took great pleasure in the fact that he could disarm her so easily. Whatever the case, when she granted him his insisted-upon five minutes after lunch he was going to get a piece of her mind—whether the lovely Caroline was with him or not!

*   *   *

'You were right, the meal was first class. I won't hesitate in recommending this place to my friends.'

Liz would put out the flags and arrange a fly-past by the Red Devils, no doubt. Walking out onto the square paved patio at the back of the restaurant, where tubs of autumnal blooms lent a sweet fragrance to the air, Emma shifted from one foot to the other, eager for Piers to rejoin his lady friend, who had popped into the washroom to freshen her make-up. 'What is it you want, Mr Redfield? You can see we're busy and I don't think my employers will be too happy with me wasting time out here when I should be working.'

He stood unflinching, his expression remaining maddeningly enigmatic as though nothing she said or did could faze him in the slightest. 'It's been my experience that most restaurants welcome my patronage with open arms, sweetheart. I don't think your employers are going to kick up a fuss if I steal you away for a few minutes. Do you?'

But Emma didn't want to be stolen away...not by anyone. And certainly not by this particular man, who seemed to cast some sort of seductive spell on her just by looking at her. No man had a right to possess such searching, dazzling blue eyes, she thought resentfully, or to smell and look so good that a girl couldn't help thinking that she'd wandered onto the glossy magazine pages of the lifestyles of the rich and famous. 'All right, then,' Emma conceded, her arms crossing her chest to keep out the cold. 'You've got your precious few minutes. Why did you want to see me?'

'I'm going away for the weekend to Paris on business. I'd very much like you to come with me.'

Emma decided she'd misheard him. Her brain was so scrambled by the fact this man could have any interest in her at all that she thought she'd imagined his startling invitation.

'I beg your pardon?'

She was delightful and gorgeous, Piers thought with heat as he gazed hungrily into her liquid brown eyes. And if he didn't have some time alone with her soon he might—just might—lose his mind. Even the fact that she'd been sent by Lawrence to plead for money hadn't dampened his almost instantaneous attraction. And the fact that she seemed so determined to keep him at a distance merely inflamed his desire even more.

'I'm going to Paris and I'd like you to come with me.'

'In what capacity?'

Piers laughed out loud, those dazzling blue eyes of his crinkling sexily at the corners and his handsome features even more devastatingly gorgeous as he gave way to humour.

'What's so funny?' Bewildered and embarrassed, Emma dropped her arms to her sides and stared.

'I'm sorry, Emma, but you have a unique way of putting things.' He stepped closer and she had to look up to meet his suddenly more serious gaze. The scent of man and heat swirled around her, making her feel strangely weak. 'In what capacity do you think?' he drawled softly.

He expects me to be able to think? Panic flooded through her as Emma absorbed the full implications of his mildly posed question. Piers Redfield—one of the UK's richest and most eligible bachelors—wanted to take her to Paris and seduce her. The premise was so unreal that for a moment or two she couldn't find the words to reply.

'I think you're inviting the wrong girl,' she said huskily, her cheeks turning a dusky rose. 'Aren't you forgetting the lady you brought to lunch?'

'Caroline?'

'That's the one.'

'She's not my girlfriend. She's my best friend's wife and she was at a loose end today so I invited her to lunch.' *And I brought her along in the hope it would make you jealous...*

'Look, thanks for thinking of me but no. I'm not interested. I hope you have a good trip all the same.'

When Emma turned away to go back inside, Piers's good-humoured patience finally snapped. Fastening his fingers around the delicate bones of her wrist, he hauled her back to face him. 'Did you lie to me about Lawrence?' he demanded.

'What do you mean?' Her heart pounding, Emma tried to twist her wrist free.

'Is it him you want?'

'Of course not! For your information, Mr Redfield, I don't want any man! All they do is cause trouble and grief and why would I want that in my life when I'm having a hard enough time as it is already?'

The anguish that laced her words hit Piers like a lightning bolt. He abruptly dropped her wrist then watched, pained, as she rubbed at the red discoloration he'd left on her delicate white skin. 'I'm sorry.' A muscle contracted in his cheekbone, heralding his genuine remorse. 'I didn't mean to hurt you. Forgive me.'

Emma wished she didn't feel as if she was going to burst into tears, but she did. 'It's all right. I mark easily, that's all.'

'It's not all right! People sue for far less, as I'm sure you're aware.'

Swallowing hard, Emma studied his pained, angry expression and something told her that it got to him the way some people wanted to take advantage of his wealth and position. It probably made it hard for him to trust even his closest friends sometimes.

'Well, I don't sue, so please don't worry on that score.' Automatically she put her hand out to touch his sleeve and almost immediately felt the steely muscles of his arm tense beneath the expensive material of his suit. One minute she was transfixed by the sudden urgent longing in his eyes and the next she was in his arms, her mouth claimed hungrily in a hard, hot kiss that seemed to melt all the bones in her body and sent her mind into a heady, tumbling spin. The touch of his lips then his tongue invading her scalded Emma like searing flames. A little desperately she shoved at his chest, but her efforts were pathetically ineffectual as her senses succumbed to the passion and need of that highly erotic stolen kiss.

'Let me go.' Dazedly staring up into the stunning blue depths of Piers's gaze, Emma knew a dazzling, shimmering moment out of time—one she'd never forget—and her fingers curled possessively into his lapels, even as she brokenly articulated the contradictory words. Her mind told her to do one thing and her body another. She'd felt the manifestation of his arousal pressing deep into the apex of her thighs and her feelings had been so wild and hot in response that she had been shaken to her core. She was practically struck dumb with the power of them. This wasn't the Emma Robards she knew. There was nothing self-contained and reserved about the way she reacted to this man's touch.

Caressing her lips one more time before stepping away, Piers shuddered, making Emma realise it had been no easy task for him to release her. Briefly he adjusted the knot of his tie, his lips hitching in a totally unapologetic little smile before he twitched his suit cuffs level with the ones on his crisp white shirt.

'You taste sweeter than the *crème brûlé* I had for dessert. I don't normally get cravings for sugar but in your case I'd definitely make an exception.'

Reaching into his inside jacket pocket, he brought out a blue and white envelope with a well-known airline's first-class insignia on it. Without preamble he handed it to her. 'Come to Paris,' he said, eyes glittering. 'I'll meet you in the VIP lounge at seven o'clock Saturday morning.'

Emma was still staring down at the envelope several minutes after he'd left.

She packed and then unpacked, sat on the bed with her head in her hands then in desperation rang Liz.

'What do you mean you don't think you should go?' Liz's normally evenly toned voice suddenly increased in volume. Her employer and friend had been hugely excited when Emma told her of Piers's invitation, and had urged her to accept it. Emma wished she could feel half as excited. What she felt right now was closer to terror than excitement. Twirling a silky brown strand of hair around her finger, she stared at her grandmother's patchwork quilt covering her bed and thought how preposterous it was that a man like Piers could possibly be interested in a girl like her. He was a corporate genius and millionaire and she was a waitress. She wasn't the kind of girl men said, 'Come to Paris' to—at least, not until now. She was the kind of girl men told their problems to, then maybe as an afterthought tried to take to bed as a sort of consolation prize—like Lawrence. The fact that she'd been ready to promise to be Piers's love slave for life when he had kissed her at the restaurant didn't alter the fact that she wasn't the kind of woman he usually took out. His dates would be beautiful, sophisticated women used to travel and luxury—who knew all the right things to say in any situation, who knew how to please and flatter a man and how to dress appropriately. What did Emma know of any of these things? It was a whole other world and one she wasn't sure she was so ready to step into—even on a short trip to Paris.

'Liz, I hardly know the man.'

'But he likes you—that's evident. He wouldn't have found out where you work and come here not once, but twice to see you! He's a respectable businessman with a solid reputation. Do you imagine that I'd let him near you for one second if I suspected that wasn't the case? I don't think you have anything to fear from him, I honestly don't.'

Remembering the way he'd kissed her, Emma silently begged to differ. Ever since it had happened she'd been feeling as if she'd been kissed awake from some kind of drugged sleep. Afterwards the world suddenly appeared so much sharper and in focus.

'We won't have anything in common,' she said, frowning.

'I wouldn't bet on that if I were you,' Liz replied knowingly.

'I was hoping you'd talk me out of it, not encourage me!'

'Emma, when are you going to start to live a little? You're a wonderful girl and I love you to bits but you can't stay being a waitress forever, taking care of your grandmother. Your loyalty and kindness are commendable but your youth is passing you by! You need to take opportunities where they come and grab them with both hands. I've already been on the phone to Fleur in Paris and she's so excited for you. She wants you to meet up if you can so be sure to ring her when you get to your hotel.'

The hotel. That was another thing. If she went to Paris

with Piers she was in effect agreeing to sleep with him—to share a bed. The very idea brought her out in a sweat. What would he expect from her? Her experience with men was limited to say the least. Up until this point in her life she'd told herself she was happy to keep it that way, but then she hadn't bargained for sexual desire so acute it was like a force of nature she was powerless to resist. Why else was she even contemplating going on this trip with him? She shouldn't be ashamed that she had needs…womanly needs that hadn't been satisfied in a very long time. There, she'd admitted it. Oh, lord! How could she possibly contemplate spending a weekend with such a powerful, sophisticated man?

Fleur. She was the anchor that Emma could hold on to should things go awry. Just knowing her best friend would be close by put a whole new complexion on the situation. 'You're right,' she said to Liz. 'I should go, shouldn't I?'

'You'll have a great time. See how the other half lives! And if you need me or Adam we're right on the end of the phone, you know that, don't you?'

'I appreciate it, Liz. Thanks.'

'Have you told your gran you're going?'

Emma released her curled-up hair from her finger to trace a pattern on one of the patchwork squares instead. 'She was pleased for me. Excited. Glad that I was going to be doing something else this weekend rather than looking after her. Her neighbour, Pam, is going to pop in from time to time the way she does during the week when I'm at work. She's told me she'll be fine.'

'And so she will be,' Liz agreed. 'She loves you so much, Emma. Of course she wants you to go and have a good time.'

'I'll see you at the restaurant Monday evening, then.'

'Don't worry if you're late back or your plans change. Just give me a ring to let me know and we'll cover it.'

Checking the time on his watch, Piers frowned. A second later, he checked it again. Pacing the VIP lounge at Heathrow like an expectant father waiting outside the maternity ward, he deliberately blanked the curious looks of the handful of other passengers that had gathered in the plush waiting-room to await the announcement of their flight. Would she come or wouldn't she? Three days had gone by since he'd seen her and he hadn't had a phone call in the interim to say she *wasn't* coming. He'd briefed Fiona, his PA, that he might get a call from an 'Emma Robards,' and if he did she was to put it through straight away—even if he was in a meeting. But no such call had come through and Piers had held on to that fact like some kind of good omen.

But now as the time drew nearer and nearer to the arrival of his flight, he found himself doubting his previous confidence. The feeling was completely new to him as far as the opposite sex was concerned, and he hated it. It made him feel vulnerable somehow, and that was definitely a feeling he was unaccustomed to. Piers Redfield admitting to feelings of vulnerability? It was akin to some pumped-up twenty-stone weightlifter admitting he had a feminine side.

Tension eating into his shoulders, he vividly recalled the sensation of Emma's supple, curvaceous body in his arms and angrily bit back his growing frustration. The uniquely bewitching taste of her delectable lips had almost brought him to his knees and the way she'd trembled in response to his kiss yet had opened to him as if he were already her lover had just been the biggest turn-on. He readily admitted to himself that this particular trip would be missing the most essential ingredient if Emma decided not to show up, and would be all the duller and more lacklustre for it. Paris was meant for lovers, not single businessmen with a bad case of unrequited lust. Glancing towards the long glass corridor beyond the room doors, he saw Miles, his driver, quicken his pace as he drew nearer. Preparing to be disappointed, Piers gave the man a curt nod as he came into the room.

'Miss Robards has just checked in, Mr Redfield. A steward will be bringing her along shortly.'

'Thank you, Miles.' Feeling like a stranded climber who had just seen the search and rescue helicopter hovering above, Piers gave a broad smile. For the first time that morning he could relax. Deciding to take advantage of the comfortable seating, he carefully shook out his precisely folded copy of the *Financial Times* to read while he waited for Emma to show.

CHAPTER FIVE

HER heart was galloping so fast, Emma feared for her ability to stay upright as she approached the VIP lounge with the steward. All the way to the airport that morning she'd anguished about whether to go or stay and in the end she'd taken a decisive deep breath and decided to live a little, as her friend had advised. But when she saw Piers fold his newspaper and rise to greet her, she almost turned and ran back the way she'd come.

How could it be possible that one man could generate so much hope and excitement inside her and at the same time so much anxiety? And why did his eyes have to be such a break-your-heart blue that there was nowhere for Emma to hide from them even if she wanted to? There was an aura about him that was almost palpable. An aura that surely came from wearing the mantle of authority as though you were born to it. Even his suit—beautifully tailored yet understated—had the mark of importance about it. Glancing down at her simple yet classic black V-necked sweater and skirt beneath the long camel-coloured coat she'd bought in last year's winter sale, Emma prayed she wouldn't disgrace him with her lack of a designer wardrobe. She loved beautiful clothes as much as the next woman but a waitress's salary didn't stretch to such things. Feeding herself, meeting her bills and ensuring that her grandmother didn't go without necessities were far more important.

Piers stood smiling as the young uniformed steward held

open the door for Emma and wished her a very pleasant
flight before smartly departing.

'You came,' he said gruffly, his glance swiftly assessing
the soft blush of colour on her cheeks.

'I don't know why,' she replied, lower lip trembling. A
ripple of pleasure and need coursed through Piers's bloodstream and anticipation simmered inside him, eager to be
gratified. With her shining eyes and beautiful face, she
reminded him of a young doe—ready to bolt at any second
if he got too near. The last thing Piers wanted to do was
scare her. He was an experienced man of the world, and
Emma was a babe in arms in comparison. She might possess the chutzpah to inveigle her way into his office but
that didn't mean she was automatically equipped to deal
with situations that were potentially intimidating. He
would have to tread very carefully. Even so, Piers couldn't
deny the pleasure he would receive from introducing her
to the delights and adventure of a weekend in one of the
most delightful cities in the world.

'Have you been to Paris before?' he asked conversationally.

'Once. My friend Fleur works in one of the Paris fashion
houses and when she first moved there I travelled with her
to help her settle into her apartment. Unfortunately we
were so busy unpacking suitcases and boxes and buying
stuff for the flat that I didn't really get time to sightsee.
But I always promised myself I'd come back one day and
see some of the things I'd missed.'

'Good. A short amount of time will be devoted to my
work, unfortunately, but my driver, Miles, is coming with
us so a car will be at your disposal to take you anywhere
you wish to go. I will, however, endeavour to conclude
my business just as soon as I can...then I'll be all yours.'

Emma's mouth went slack. If he had meant to reassure

her, his words had the opposite effect. Now she trembled even worse than before. She tried to smile but somehow that was like trying to smile when you were abseiling down the side of a mountain at full pelt. 'Good. I—I mean, thank you for arranging the car and everything. You won't mind if I go visit my friend?'

'Sweetheart, Miles will take you wherever you want to go and wait for you to bring you back to the hotel. Just don't stay away too long, will you? I'm looking forward to us sharing some time together.' Placing his hand on the pure wool lapel of her coat, Piers stroked it, the little gesture oddly seductive, and suddenly Emma's legs felt as weak as a kitten's. The effect of this man's touch was tumultuous and instant and created the most unsettling riot of sensation in her body and her heart. How on earth was she going to survive a weekend in the most intimate of circumstances with such a man? And more to the point— would she be able to cope with the aftermath when she returned to the real world?

It wasn't in the realms of Emma's experience to walk into the lobby of one of the most luxurious hotels in Paris and find herself intimately acquainted with eighteenth-century décor in the style of Louis XV, with Italian marble floors and Baccarat crystal chandeliers. While Piers registered at one of the several individual reception desks, Emma stood in awe, feeling like a character from a fairy tale who had just stumbled upon a cave full of untold treasure. Observing the other occupants of the opulent reception area, she saw people going about their business as if this was everyday, like visiting the supermarket for groceries. Nobody appeared as awed or nervous as she felt, and she told herself she must stick out like a sore thumb while Piers blended in with the rest of them like a prince used to living in a palace. Only he didn't quite blend in. The man had too much charisma and presence for that. Even now, the attractive receptionist with her awesomely perfect chignon and faultlessly applied make-up was smiling prettily up at something Piers had said, her body language revealing that she wasn't immune to the charm and good looks that made him stand out from the crowd.

And neither was Emma. She'd spent almost the entire plane journey feeling overwhelmed. Not just by the luxury and 'specialness' of travelling first class for the first time in her entire life, but by the fact that she was accompanying one of the most attractive men she'd ever been acquainted with—on a trip to Paris, as romantic a destination as one could wish to find. All she could do was stare out the window and wonder what other astounding events fate had in store for her.

'Emma.'

Sucking in a breath sharply, Emma picked up her green and tan suitcase, straightened the strap of her brown leather bag more comfortably on her shoulder, then moved gingerly across the dazzling white marble in her unaccustomed high heels to join Piers at the desk.

'Leave the suitcase. The bellhop will bring the luggage up to our suite.' Briefly touching the back of her waist, his glance was concerned and intimate and for a terrifying moment Emma was unable to tear her own glance away. Somewhere in the back of her mind she registered the words 'our suite' and just about managed to keep her feet on the ground and not pick up her suitcase and flee.

'Are you OK?'

'Fine. This place is beautiful, isn't it?'

Right now, as far as Piers was concerned, it couldn't hold a candle to Emma. With her petal-soft skin and beguiling features—not to mention the innate grace with which she carried herself—the woman was quite simply stunning. And if he'd been impressed by her demeanour before, he was even more so now after travelling with her. Granted he'd had to work on his laptop for most of the journey, but she hadn't bent his ear with inconsequential chatter as some other women of his acquaintance would. She'd been quite content to relax and stare out of the window, then flick through the glossy fashion magazines that he'd instructed Miles to purchase for her at the airport shop. They'd had some conversation over breakfast on the plane but even then Piers quickly realised that Emma wasn't a woman who needed constant attention. She was remarkably self-contained for someone of her years. It didn't surprise him that his son should find her so easy to confide in.

'We'll go up to the suite and freshen up, then I'm afraid I'm going to have to leave you for a few hours to amuse yourself. I'll be back later on this afternoon then perhaps we can take a walk and see some of the sights together?'

Strolling along at leisure on a crisply cold winter's day was one of Emma's favourite pastimes too, and where better to do it than in a cosmopolitan, elegant city like Paris?

'I'd like that.' Sensing her skin grow hot as his gaze idly drifted over her face, Emma wished she knew how to control her embarrassment more easily. If Piers expected her to act the sophisticate in any way, the man was bound to be disappointed. That said, she wasn't a total philistine. People were her business, after all. In the restaurant trade, the one attribute that came top of the list of requirements in providing good service was knowing how to deal with people from all walks of life. 'Keep the customer happy and they'll come back—maybe even bring their friends.' She'd like a pound for every time Liz or Adam had expounded that particular little homily.

'Good.'

Mere words were hardly adequate to describe the suite of rooms that they had been allocated by the hotel. Hardly batting an eyelid as he undid his suit jacket and loosened his tie, Piers seemed to take the grandeur of their opulent surroundings as his due. As Emma stood transfixed just inside the door, her new high-heeled shoes pinching her toes, her glance fell on the plumply cushioned gold wing-backed chairs either side of the marble fireplace, then drifted around the room, examining every antique lamp, every candlestick and every gilt-framed painting as though she stood in a museum admiring the artefacts. It was just like being a child again. She could almost imagine her mother stooping down beside her, whispering, 'You can look, but don't touch.' As she bit her lip at the memory, her gaze somehow stumbled back to Piers.

'Why don't you take off those shoes?' he suggested lightly. 'Rest your feet while you have the chance.'

Her slender black-stockinged legs looked amazing in the black stilettos with their dainty little criss-crossed straps, but Piers had known from the off that they were killing her. Smiling a little sheepishly, she nudged one shoe off with the toe of the other, then stood in her stockinged feet looking as if someone had just given her the key to heaven. Piers's desire was instantaneous, tightening his groin and heating his skin flame-hot so that he had to move away to conceal his sudden arousal. Inwardly he cursed the fact that he had to go to a meeting across town and would be away for at least three hours, maybe more. Now he'd got her alone, he was frustrated and impatient that he couldn't take her to bed straight away. If he had his way, they wouldn't see any of the sights of Paris the whole weekend other than this suite. But as much as the idea turned him on, he knew it wouldn't be entirely fair to Emma to bring her to such a beautiful city and not let her see some of its famous landmarks. So Piers would go to his meeting, let Miles take her wherever she wanted to go and when he returned to the hotel later he would take her for a long, romantic walk around the city, deriving great pleasure from introducing her to some of the sights and places that he'd long been familiar with.

'You must be a mind-reader.'

'If only that were true—it would make my work a whole lot easier, I can tell you.'

'I'm sorry you have to work while we're here.' Hesitating over expressing such a revealing sentiment, Emma turned away before she could gauge Piers's expression.

'You couldn't possibly be as sorry as I am, sweetheart. But I'll make it up to you later... That's a promise.'

As she swung her gaze back to his, Emma insides tightened at the irrefutable flare of longing in Piers's fascinating blue eyes.

'I'd suggest you wear something more comfortable on your feet if you're going sightseeing,' he said, slightly rough-voiced, then moved across the sumptuous carpet to the door that the bellhop had explained led to the bedroom. 'I've instructed Miles to take you wherever you want to go, and he'll pay for whatever you need. I have only one stipulation...'

Emma raised her eyebrow. 'What's that?'

'Enjoy yourself. That's an order.' And before Emma could tell him that she had money of her own, that she preferred to be independent and would pay her own way as much as possible, he disappeared inside the door and shut it behind him.

She found a pleasant and good-humoured ally in Miles, Piers's chauffeur. From the east end of London, he was as chatty and as jovial as one of that city's famed taxi drivers, littering his conversations with amusing anecdotes about the places he'd been with his employer and the people he'd met from all walks of life. He was also well acquainted with the French city and seemed to know its back streets and wide avenues like the back of his hand. When Emma expressed her nervousness about going up to the top of the Eiffel Tower on her own, he quickly agreed to accompany her. But even with his reassuring presence, Emma hardly dared look down as, ensconced in one of the tower's two working elevators, they ascended higher and higher up its intricate, lace-like iron structure. At the top, she took her courage in both hands and stared down at the panoramic view of the city in awed wonder.

'Now, how's that for a sight for sore eyes?' Miles teased gently beside her.

'It's fantastic,' Emma breathed, brown eyes shining. Looking on like a doting father, Miles smiled with deep satisfaction. He could quite see why his illustrious boss was indisputably taken with this particular young lady. If he'd been twenty years younger and not so happily married to Veronica, he'd be quite taken with her himself. Pretty as a picture she was, with her soft chestnut-brown hair and sparkling dark eyes. And she wasn't aloof, not like some of Piers's other lady friends who thought they were so much better than they were. Quite content working for the man the papers dubbed a corporate genius, Miles knew he would enjoy this trip even more than usual because of the affability and sweetness of Emma Robards.

She had lunch with Fleur. She'd invited Miles to join them in the bustling sidewalk bistro not far from the Place de la Concorde where their hotel was situated but he'd politely declined, told her where she could find him when she was ready to leave, then discreetly made himself scarce. Excited and happy to be with the friend she had known since her schooldays, Emma hugged the petite and pretty Fleur then sat opposite her across the wrought-iron table and caught up with everything that had been happening since Emma had seen her last.

'And now you must tell me your news,' Fleur insisted after a while. 'I especially want to know about the man you're with. Mum's told me that he's utterly gorgeous, loaded and single and that he came into the restaurant twice looking for you. Things like that don't happen every day. Talk about kismet!'

'Fleur, I—'

'Where are you staying, by the way? Somewhere swish, I hope?'

Amused at her friend's excitement, Emma told her and Fleur released a long, low whistle. 'He's got taste as well as money! That's only about the best hotel in Paris, Em. You need a small fortune just to have coffee there!'

Raising her glass of mineral water to her lips, Emma couldn't prevent the wave of heat that washed over her. Her friend seemed perfectly accepting of the fact that Emma was here in Paris with a man she'd barely known for five minutes—sharing a suite with him at a luxurious hotel with all that that situation entailed. For a few unsettling moments Emma couldn't help but question the mad impulse that had made her go through with such a thing...and then she thought about Piers himself and automatically pressed her thighs closer together beneath her simple black skirt. *Desire.* That was what had driven her to undertake this trip. Even though the mere idea terrified the life out of her, when it came down to the most basic of reasons, she'd come to Paris to let Piers Redfield seduce her.

'I— He's nice.' Shrugging, she was painfully aware that of all the adjectives she could have chosen to describe

Piers Redfield, 'nice' was the most ineffectual and inappropriate one of all. Dynamic, gorgeous, sex-on-legs, perhaps even a little ruthless—now, if Emma had used those she'd be getting somewhere.

Her friend was also affronted by such a lame description. 'Nice?' Fleur made a face. 'You could have worked for MI5, you know? When it comes to getting information out of you I'd get more joy from someone deaf, dumb and blind! Give me a break, Em. Who is he? What's his name? How did you meet? More to the point—how do you feel about the man? And if you don't come up with satisfactory answers soon, I'm not going to give you the perfectly gorgeous little black dress I managed to wangle out of my employer specially for you!'

'Oh, Fleur, you didn't! You shouldn't!' Overwhelmed by her friend's generosity, Emma stared for the first time at the beautifully printed cream and gold bag that Fleur had tucked beneath her chair.

'I won't, unless you spill the beans in three seconds flat!'

After just a few short hours, Emma pronounced herself in love with the city. With its elegantly faded patina, the buildings of Paris easily reminding her of so many paintings, she was utterly enchanted. No wonder artists past and present found such inspiration there. After leaving Fleur, and clutching the unexpected gift of the beautiful little black dress, Emma asked Miles to take her to the famous Louvre museum, once a medieval castle and now transformed into the largest museum in the world. She was suitably impressed by the glass pyramid entrance that was just a foretaste of the treasures to come inside. At her insistence, Miles accompanied her and they both stood awestruck in admiration along with other silent visitors to pay due homage to the *Mona Lisa*.

After almost three hours walking around just one of the vast wings that held some of the huge collection of exhibits, Emma's feet started to protest, even in her sensible shoes. At Miles' suggestion they drove back to the hotel so that she could rest for a while and wait for Piers's return. As trepidatious as that made her feel, Emma couldn't deny that she needed a break. As well as rising ridiculously early that morning, she'd lain awake half the night fretting over the wisdom of going to Paris with a man she hardly knew.

When she let herself into their suite, her heart almost stalled in her chest when she saw Piers lounging in one of the luxurious wing-back chairs, a magazine on his lap and a glass of iced water set down on the beautiful antique occasional table beside him. Immediately that crystalline blue gaze of his in all its unsettling, provocative intensity attached itself to Emma and wouldn't let go.

'Hello.' Her words felt like prisoners trapped in her throat and she struggled to set them free. 'I didn't think you'd be back yet. How did your meeting go?'

Her face looked a little rosy from the fresh air outside, her soft brown hair was prettily mussed and her expression was all eyes. Just like a little girl, accidentally stumbling upon a place she'd been warned not to venture into yet couldn't resist. One glance at her angelic face and Piers was immediately and heavily aroused. All through the tedium of his meeting he'd had more than half his mind on the girl he'd brought to Paris, and when the gathering of international board members drew to a thankful close he'd found himself in a state of almost agonising anticipation at the idea of seeing Emma again. Of having her all to himself for the rest of the weekend... Now he rose to his feet, stripped off his tie, threw it on a chair and unbuttoned his waistcoat, and through all of those actions never once took his eyes off the girl still standing by the door.

'The meeting was tedious but necessary, I'm afraid.' He shrugged, advancing slowly across the room towards Emma as he spoke. 'How have you been enjoying Paris? What have you been up to, hmm?'

Swallowing hard, Emma managed a nervous smile. 'I've had a wonderful time. Miles and I went up the Eiffel Tower, then I had lunch with my friend Fleur. After that Miles took me to the Louvre to see the *Mona Lisa*. Piers, it was so beautiful! Oh, and I took my shoes off because my feet were aching and one of the invigilators told me off and I had to put them back on. We only came back to give my feet a rest because I've walked so much. Oh!'

She gasped when Piers stepped forward and started to ease her coat off her shoulders. Emma immediately dropped the carrier bag containing her new dress.

'Give me your coat. That's better. Kick off your shoes and come and sit down. Where is Miles now?' Laying her coat on the back of the ornate gold chaise longue, Piers turned back to admire her figure in her simple black skirt and sweater, his gaze gravitating to the gentle swell of her breasts beneath the black wool with a hunger he could hardly contain. Just now when he'd helped her off with her coat, the heady, sensual fragrance of her perfume had merely compounded the effect of her on his heightened libido and it was all Piers could do to stay just this close to civilised. In all his experience with women, he'd never been so acutely and passionately aroused.

Folding her arms self-consciously across her chest, Emma tried to look anywhere but at Piers. But it was practically impossible to wrench her gaze free from those burning blue eyes of his—like trying not to crave chocolate

when you were on a diet... From the moment she'd set
eyes on him every cell in her body had been given an
injection of energy. All the sights of Paris paled into in-
significance when she looked at this man. He was so out
of Emma's league in every way, yet it was impossible for
her to deny the fact that she desired him above all other
men. Now as he stood there, tall, tanned and undeniably
gorgeous, every inch the dynamic, powerful businessman,
Emma thought: This can't be happening to me. Not plain
Emma Jane Robards. There must be some mistake.

He'll break your heart, a small voice warned inside her,
but Emma knew she was way past the point where she
would heed it.

'Miles has gone back to his hotel room. He said to—to
phone him if you needed anything.'

Thoughtfully silent for a few moments, Piers strolled
across the room to the old-fashioned cream and gold telephone seated atop a polished bureau and raised the receiver
to his ear. *'Bonjour.'*

With not much more than schoolgirl French to get by
on, Emma surprised herself by understanding that Piers
had asked not to be disturbed for the next couple of hours
at least. As the receiver was replaced carefully back on its
rest, her heart started to pound alarmingly.

With bated breath she stared at Piers for explanation.

'Do you need anything?' he asked her, his intense
glance making it almost impossible for her to move.

Her brow puckering, Emma lifted her shoulders in confusion. 'I— Do I need anything? I don't know what you
mean.'

'OK...now ask me the same question.'

Emma finally understood. Her tongue cleaving to the
roof of her mouth, she took a deep, shuddering breath to
give herself courage then looped her softly mussed hair

behind her ears with trembling hands. 'Is there any-thing…you need, Piers?'

Relief and desire warring for precedence, Piers nodded slowly. 'Yes, sweetheart. Right now I badly need to touch you.'

CHAPTER SIX

HARDLY knowing what she was about, Emma started to move towards the bedroom door. 'You know what?' she said breathlessly. 'I really should unpack and get myself sorted out. Do you mind?'

'I've already had a maid come up and do that.' Two steps behind her, Piers was in turn frustrated and amused by her haste to put some distance between them. Halfway into the bedroom with its glorious red and amber silk canopy draped above the French-style bed, Emma spun around in genuine alarm. 'You had a maid come up and unpack for me?'

Her first thought was that she wasn't entirely sure she liked the idea of some stranger going through her clothing, probably thumbing her nose up at Emma's non-designer apparel, and no doubt jumping to all sorts of unwanted conclusions about her relationship with Piers.

'You'd already gone out and I didn't think you'd want your clothes left lying creased in a suitcase.'

'Thank you.' His calm explanation immediately took the wind out of Emma's sails but still left her flustered and ill-prepared to deal with what was going on. 'That was thoughtful of you.'

'Why are you trying to run away from me?'

'I'm not!'

Assessing her panic-stricken expression from the other side of the beautiful, elegant bed, Piers couldn't help but smile. The girl fascinated and excited him more than any other woman had in the longest time. Along with her natural beauty there was an artlessness about her that led Piers to believe that artifice just wasn't part of her make-up—even if she had somehow contrived to get into his office without being caught. As far as he knew she hadn't lied to anyone to get there. He was a little jaded with women who acted like men in the bedroom stakes, and Emma's charming innocence was a refreshing change.

'Do I frighten you?' he asked reasonably.

'No. I mean yes… I mean, I don't know.' Once she'd had some intelligence; now she was acting like an idiot. Emma wished she could stop shaking. How was it that this man was able to reduce her to a mumbling jelly in his presence when she was used to dealing with all kinds of difficult people at the restaurant? Even overenthusiastic young men who'd had too much wine to drink and decided that Emma must be part of the menu too. They got short shrift from their previously polite waitress, along with a stern lecture on how to behave properly in public. But Piers Redfield… He was a challenge she'd never imagined being faced with in a million years. Just thinking about who he was and the awesome reputation that preceded him was enough to make Emma quake—let alone entertaining the very real possibility that they might make love!

'I don't want to frighten you, Emma. I just want us to get better acquainted. Is that all right with you?'

As far as Emma was concerned, that was like asking her if she wanted to throw herself out of a plane without a parachute. She was so overwhelmed it made her dizzy. As Piers drew near, she mused that it was highly unfair that one man seemed to possess so many advantages but at the same time was perversely glad that he did. His expensive cologne lingered around him in a potent mix of virile heat and sexual edge. His hard, well-defined jaw clearly denoted he took no prisoners and the more deeply tanned skin just at the base of his throat where he'd freed the top button of his impeccable white shirt was somehow erotically tantalising, along with the relentlessly blue eyes that blazed back at her so hotly.

Emma wondered how a girl was supposed to withstand such a sensual onslaught without losing her mind. When it came to matters of sex and seduction, she'd barely left the starting block. Her economics lecturer, Richard—the one she'd had the disastrous love affair with—had proclaimed himself 'infatuated' with her *naiveté,* but would Piers find it remotely charming in the same way? Her insides tightened unbearably and she had to remind herself to breathe as Piers laid a hand on the softly accentuated curve of her hip and with very little force impelled her against him. His touch provoked such violent trembling throughout Emma's body that she was certain he must hear her teeth chatter. Finding her already exquisitely tender breasts up close and personal against the iron wall of his chest, she tipped up her chin to find her sharply released breath mingling with his, her gaze suddenly imprisoned by the wry little twist at the corner of his highly appealing mouth.

'All I've been able to think about all day is kissing you,' he confessed hoarsely. Emma wanted to reply, 'Me too,' but speech was a faculty that had apparently deserted her. The man's sexual potency undid her and now that he was so close her imagination was running riot with all the things she wanted him to do to her. Made helpless by desire, Emma tentatively touched her lips to his. They were firm yet soft and just one little taste yielded such a powerful explosion of primeval longing that everything inside her seemed to melt.

'I'm not a schoolboy,' Piers rasped, his voice growing more commanding as his hands slid down her ribcage to clasp her hips. 'Now kiss me properly.' Unfazed by the reprimand, Emma kissed him on a sigh, her mouth opening helplessly as the bounds of self-restraint broke, willingly allowing his tongue to probe and demand and fill her hotly with the taste of one very virile and aroused male. Then, acquainting himself with the delectable contours of her delightful bottom through the smooth fabric of her skirt, Piers worked the material as far up as her panties then smoothly slipped his hand between her thighs. The effect on Emma was immediate and all-consuming. A blaze of erotic heat spread throughout her body like an unstoppable fire, making her quiver in his arms even more.

Her damp, silken heat almost undid Piers. Almost painfully aroused, he blessed the fates for the powerful sexual attraction that erupted like a chemical explosion between them. She was so responsive—exquisitely so. But that being the case, something told him that Emma was still comparatively innocent—quite unlike any other woman he'd made love to before. The way she trembled so violently in his arms confirmed his suspicions, even as it turned him on. His seduction of her would be all the sweeter for her lack of experience, he decided—even more satisfying would be the fact that his son had been unable to seduce her first. No matter what Emma had said, Piers couldn't believe for one second that Lawrence hadn't tried to get her into bed. What man with a pulse wouldn't?

'Piers?'

'Hmm?'

Reluctantly withdrawing his lips from hers, Piers gazed down into Emma's beautiful face.

Her dark eyes dazed and beguiling—soft clouds of hazel-brown—her tender mouth plundered and moistened by his passionate kisses, Emma adjusted her clothing and stared nervously up at Piers. 'I think—I think you're going a little fast for me.' Blushing profusely, she lowered her gaze, shocked and surprised when Piers lifted her chin and forced her to look at him.

'What are you frightened of, Emma? You must have known this was why I brought you to Paris.'

When she didn't immediately reply but chewed down anxiously on her softly plump lower lip instead, Piers's blue eyes blazed with frustration as his brain tried to absorb the silent signal she was giving him. 'Just how much experience have you had, Emma?'

Apprehension and panic tightened Emma's throat. 'I'm not a virgin, if that's what you mean.'

That wasn't what Piers meant at all. Desire still ebbing powerfully through him, he strode across the room and back again, hardly able to trust himself to speak. Surely she couldn't be confused or surprised about his desire for her? Hadn't he amply demonstrated his fierce attraction? But sweet, comparatively innocent and only twenty-five, Emma was an unknown quantity and right now he had to be certain she knew where she stood with him if things were to proceed to a satisfactory conclusion.

'But this isn't something you do very often…is that what you're telling me?'

Hot colour stained her cheeks and her big brown eyes looked indisputably wounded.

Damn.

'My last relationship was about six years ago if you must know and that only lasted three months because I found out that he was married with children. And, in answer to your question—no, this isn't something I do very often. If you were expecting some kind of experienced *femme fatale* then I'm sorry that I've disappointed you. No doubt you're regretting inviting me on this trip.'

'On the contrary. All I want to do now is make sure

you know where you stand with me. Perhaps it's just as well you called a halt to things when you did. I feel I should at least be honest with you before we go any further. I don't want you to imagine that this is the start of something more…meaningful than it is.'

Had she at any point been hoping for something more than an illicit weekend in Paris? Emma tried hard to think straight over the disorienting thud of her heartbeat. She wasn't in the market for a more meaningful relationship either, and up until now recreational sex had been something that other girls might indulge in but Emma certainly didn't. That was why she'd suddenly felt panic when things seemed to be veering out of control with Piers. Oh, why did she have to be so scared? Just because lovemaking with her ex had been such an unsatisfactory, almost bitter experience, it didn't mean she was destined to suffer a repeat of that with Piers. Already she was more aroused by his kisses than she had ever been by Richard's hasty and graceless fumblings. If only she could let go of that rigid control she'd assumed so long ago. She was an adult now and shouldn't be ashamed that she had needs of a sexual nature, but suppressing them had become such a habit that Emma wondered if she'd ever truly be able to surrender to them without feeling that she'd be hurt as a consequence.

Now, because of her hesitation, Piers was making her feel as if she was some silly adolescent girl who didn't know the rules in this adult game and for some reason felt compelled to spell them out for her. It was a complete mistake her coming to Paris with him at all, Emma decided, and at this precise moment she was mere inches away from packing her suitcase and going home.

'I know where I stand with you, Piers, I'm not as naïve as you think I am. I've got the message loud and clear.

You're warning me not to get any silly ideas about having a relationship with you. You brought me to Paris to sleep with me and that's all. I'm not the kind of woman you're normally interested in and I certainly don't move in the same social circles that you do, so once this is over there's no chance of us bumping into each other at any time in the future. So best not get my hopes up. Am I right?'

Normally he would be relieved at such insight but right now all Piers felt was a disagreeable pricking of his conscience—as if he'd somehow cheated her in some way. The feeling was about as welcome as a swarm of bees. Troubled by the hurt and anger swirling in her eyes, he was suddenly compelled to learn more about the girl he'd brought to Paris. Even though it was damn near killing him to staunch the blaze of lust he was feeling, he dropped down onto the bed behind him and raked his fingers irritably through his thick fair hair.

'Let's get one thing clear. It's not because you're a waitress that I wouldn't consider a relationship with you. I just don't happen to be interested in commitment, period. I was married once—to Lawrence's mother, Naomi—and suffice to say the experience made hell seem like a garden of roses in comparison. Now my associations with women are all relatively short and sweet.'

His lips quirked a rueful grin and despite her hurt Emma felt an answering tug in her belly. 'But whatever you think of me right now I can assure you I would never force you to do anything you didn't want to do. You're here because you want to be here and if you decide you don't want to be here then I won't do a damn thing to stop you leaving. You have your return ticket—you can fly back to London just as soon as a flight can be arranged. Miles would, of course, drive you to the airport. So it's up to you, Emma. What do you want to do?'

Emma decided she could handle Piers not wanting commitment. Not at any point had she deluded herself that they had a future—even without him just confirming it. She didn't want commitment either. He was way out of her league and they both knew it—even if he had taken pains to explain that Emma being a waitress had nothing to do with his not wanting a relationship. All he wanted from her was physical gratification. Men and women came to such mutually satisfying arrangements all the time, she told herself, and she wouldn't be the first girl to be seduced by an older, more successful man purely to satisfy a physical urge. So she told herself to act like a grown-up, save her wounded pride for a more appropriate situation and just give herself up to the magic of Paris. What could be so hard about that?

'I'm sorry I—that I stopped things when I did. I was— I was overwhelmed.' Her hand fluttered to her throat. 'If it's all right with you...I'd like to stay.'

'You wouldn't be here in the first place if it wasn't all right with me. I brought you to Paris because I wanted to be with you. Isn't that obvious?'

Emma clasped and unclasped her hands. 'I suppose so.'

'Then why don't you come over here and talk to me?'

'Talk to you?'

'Yes. Is the concept unfamiliar?'

Her melting dark eyes immediately wary, Emma looked as if she was wondering if she could allow herself to trust him after all. Inwardly Piers cursed. Did she think he was going to pounce on her, or something equally Neanderthal?

'What do you want to talk about?'

'You, as a matter of fact.'

'What about me?'

When she didn't make any move to join him, Piers bit back his growing frustration and told himself to get a grip on his escalating libido. Right now chairing a meeting of the sharpest, most astute business minds in Europe seemed a hundred times easier. 'Were you in love with the guy who was married?'

'No.' Remembering the passionless—at least on her part—relationship she'd shared with Richard, Emma had no hesitation in stating the truth. The plain fact of the matter was she had caved in to persuasion when she'd been at a low ebb. Still reeling from the sudden death of her mother three months earlier, at nineteen she'd practically thrown away her virginity on the first man who'd been really determined to woo her. The fact that that particular man had turned out to be a liar and cheat was just her bad luck, or poor judgement, as the case might be. She certainly hadn't lost any sleep over him since then—except maybe to regret it bitterly.

'Just "no"?'

'I don't want to talk about it. As far as memories go, it's not in my top ten of all-time greats.'

'So in six years there hasn't been anyone else? Not even the occasional lover?'

There shouldn't be so much emotion invested in her answer but it surprised Piers to realise there was. It was bad enough that he was already ridiculously jealous of the married guy—he didn't know how he was going to handle hearing about any casual relationships since. But Emma was staring down at the sumptuous gold-coloured carpet with a faraway look in her eyes that made Piers long to bring her back to the place that they'd been before she'd declared herself overwhelmed.

'We clearly move in very different worlds. These kind of liaisons may be the norm for you, but they're not for me.'

So the woman hadn't had a lover in six long years?

Were all the men in her life living in a bubble or what? Or was Emma one of those women who were secretly holding out for a young girl's romantic dream? Mr Right, house in suburbia, two-point-four children and all? Disliking the streak of cynicism that wove through him, Piers got up from the bed and walked over to her.

'I may not be in the market for happy-ever-after, but that doesn't mean I treat any of my partners with anything less than total respect. It's simply that my work is very demanding. Sometimes I can go for months without having someone in my life, and I'm a man who likes female company.'

The silence that followed bristled with meaning. When Emma reached up to sweep her hair back from her face, Piers caught her hand and did it for her, his touch making her heartbeat go wild once again.

'I want to make love to you, Emma...but only when you're ready. I'm sorry if you felt that I rushed you.' Dropping a kiss at the corner of her softly parted lips, Piers looked into her eyes with a wry little smile. 'So, how are your feet holding up?'

'My feet?'

'Think you could handle some more walking? There's a charming little café I know not far from here, and right now I could use some coffee. How about you?'

Relief vied with profound disappointment as Emma considered the question. If only she hadn't acted like a frightened little rabbit when Piers was kissing her earlier they might now be in bed together, getting better acquainted, as he had so aptly put it. Instead Emma was wound up like a coiled spring, her body aching for his touch, for the fulfilment only this man could bring. To put it mildly, she was aflame for him. Couldn't he tell by the way she trembled every time he touched her?

'Coffee sounds good to me. I'll just go and freshen up and change my shoes.'

As she hurried into the beautifully appointed marble bathroom with every conceivable luxury known to man, Piers knew a sudden longing to get out of his formal business suit and don more casual clothes—just like an ordinary tourist. As he changed, he told himself he had to be losing that famous edge he supposedly had with women. Why else would he be equally keen to take a beautiful girl for coffee in a sidewalk café instead of taking her straight to bed?

He held her hand as they walked and Emma couldn't deny the pleasure that gave her. She was amazed that such a simple thing could feel so good but everything seemed so much more intense when she was with Piers. The sights they passed on the way, the people and the sidewalk cafés all seemed like a Technicolor dream in comparison to the everyday monochrome that she'd experienced before. Stealing a glance at Piers's relaxed profile as they strolled, Emma wondered what it would be like to have a man like him as a permanent fixture in her life.

The thought came out of nowhere, and made her stomach drop as if she'd missed a step. What was she thinking of? She didn't want a man in her life, at least not in any permanent way…like a husband. Better that she lived a single life than put all her hopes in the false security of marriage when a few years down the line—maybe sooner—her husband walked out. It still hurt that her father had done just that when Emma was only nine because he was in love with another woman. Her mother's distress had left her feeling helpless and yet responsible for putting things right—even if that was impossible. But it wasn't only her mother that her father had rejected…it was Emma too. That realisation—along with the wave of pain it brought—never quite diminished no matter how hard she wished it would.

'Emma?'

'Sorry?'

'We're here.'

They were on the boulevard St-Germain, at a large café with green and gold umbrellas, where Piers had told her some of the leading writers and thinkers of the day—like Sartre and de Beauvoir—had once entranced their listeners. Emma glanced around in fascination at the well-dressed tourists and Parisians alike who occupied the tables, imagining the café as it must have been all that time ago, and a little *frisson* of pleasure danced down her spine. A waiter appeared as if by magic, and with dazzling efficiency, and a froth of quick-fire French, showed Piers and Emma to a table at the end of the row lining the pavement. When Piers had given him their order, he unbuttoned his chocolate-brown suede jacket, leant back in the wrought-iron seat and considered Emma with what she could only describe as a lazy, melting smile purely designed to get whatever he wanted from a woman. A girl would have to possess a will of iron to refuse him anything. Beneath the table Emma's knees shook as she undid her own coat and tried to appear casual about it.

'So…how are you enjoying Paris so far?' he asked her.

'It's everything I thought it would be and more. I can't believe I actually saw the *Mona Lisa!* It was incredible…absolutely breathtaking.' *Though I wish I'd seen it with you…*

'I agree—it's one thing to see it on a print or a postcard, but the real thing does leave you lost for words. I wouldn't have minded seeing it again.'

'We can go back if you like… In fact, why don't we?'

When Piers didn't immediately reply Emma bit back her

burst of enthusiasm to forlornly wonder if he found her lack of sophistication trying. Her youth and inexperience was probably starting to pall. Maybe he was wishing he'd invited someone else instead?

Seeing her crestfallen expression, Piers leaned across the table and captured her hand. 'There are lots of other experiences we can share together, Emma. In a beautiful, cosmopolitan city like this we're spoilt for choice.'

Staring down at his fingers clasping hers, at the strong, lean hands with their clean, square-cut nails, she knew a sudden moment of panic. The gulf between them seemed so immeasurably vast. He was a highly successful, wealthy businessman at the top of his game and she…well, Emma still hadn't decided on a career. Until her grandmother had had her operation and was well on the road to recovery, Emma knew there wasn't even the faintest hope of thinking about a new direction job-wise. All her concentration would be on making sure her beloved Gran had everything she needed to make her as comfortable as possible in her little house. Besides…making changes took confidence— the kind of confidence Emma didn't have at present. She'd spent the last five years caring for her ailing grandmother and frankly didn't have the energy either.

Tugging her hand free, she self-consciously lowered her gaze. 'I get a little carried away when I'm excited about things. No doubt you find it childish.'

'Not at all.'

Glancing up, Emma was startled to discover that Piers was smiling, his crystal-blue eyes unwaveringly steady as they gazed back deeply into hers. 'On the contrary, I find it utterly charming.'

CHAPTER SEVEN

OH GRAN... I'm in so much trouble you wouldn't believe.

It was just as well that the waiter appeared at that moment with their *café au lait* along with some very decadent-looking pastries that Piers had ordered. A timely distraction, as far as Emma was concerned. Every moment she spent with this man, she found it harder and harder to distance herself emotionally from what was going on between them. No matter how often she told herself that once he slept with her she would in all probability never set eyes on him again, a glimmering of hope had foolishly surfaced in her heart that things might turn out differently. A renegade thought that needed reining in as quickly as possible...

'Tell me a little bit more about yourself.' His expression relaxed, Piers moved his coffee-cup towards him. 'How long have you been waitressing?'

'Six years.' Lifting her pastry off the delicately patterned side-plate, Emma took a small, careful bite, feeling her cheeks flush hotly even as she tried to pretend it didn't matter that Piers might find such an apparent lack of ambition extremely dull.

'I take it you must enjoy it if you've been doing it that long?'

Her soft brown eyes became instantly wary and Piers cursed himself for not finding a better way of phrasing the question. Contrary to what people might imagine, he was the last person to look down on anyone for doing a 'menial' job. The fact that Emma had been in regular employment for six years with the same employer said a lot more about her, and her loyalty to the people she worked for, than her lack of desire for a more high-profile career.

'Adam and Liz—the owners—are great to work for. They've been very good to me. And yes—I do enjoy the work. The atmosphere is lively and busy and I guess I'm just happy there.'

'You never wanted to do anything else?'

'I have thought about it. I even toyed with the idea of going back into further education but it's not that easy. I have commitments...'

'Oh?' Curious about what might be coming next, Piers took his time stirring sugar into his coffee. 'What kind of commitments?'

'My grandmother. She's my only family and she's been unwell for a long time. In just over a week she's going into hospital for an operation and I'm going to have to help take care of her until she's fully recovered. It could be several months before she's properly back on her feet again.' Wiping a smudge of powdered sugar from her pastry off her nose, Emma couldn't keep the anxious undertone from her voice.

'What's wrong with her?'

'It's her heart.' One moment she was smiling but in the next her brown eyes were brimming with tears. 'I'm sorry.' Appalled at her sudden display of emotion, Emma put down her pastry and dived frantically into her bag for a tissue.

Before she was able to find one, Piers took a perfectly pressed linen square from his inside jacket pocket and placed it in her hand. 'There's nothing to apologise for. You must love her very deeply.'

'I do. Thank you.' Sniffling into the handkerchief that smelled arrestingly of the expensive cologne Piers wore,

Emma silently lamented her inability to keep her emotions at bay. Piers couldn't possibly be interested in her troubles at home. All he wanted was a brief sexual liaison, not an emotional outpouring of how worried she was about the person who was nearest and dearest to her. He was probably wishing he could just put her on the earliest plane home and forget the whole thing, and Emma could hardly blame him. As a potential conquest, she must be a huge disappointment.

'You should try some of the pastry. It's delicious,' she said shakily, and forced a smile to cover her embarrassment.

Watching her try to repair the tell-tale signs of moisture that had dampened her cheeks, Piers was taken aback by the feelings of protectiveness that assailed him. Seriously concerned about this unexpected broadside Emma had unwittingly launched into his emotions, he just about managed to restrain himself from leaning across the table and patting her tears dry himself. Things just didn't seem to be turning out the way he'd planned at all. What he'd been planning on was a lazy, seductive afternoon in bed, after which he had hoped to persuade the lovely Emma to take a bath with him, then get ready together to go out to dinner. His dependable PA had booked them a table at one of the city's most exclusive restaurants, which only the seriously well-heeled frequented, and which Piers's previous dates had professed to love. But suddenly that particular restaurant didn't seem right for this particular girl and another smaller, quieter venue that served regional cuisine and had a superlative wine list sprang helpfully to mind. All Piers had to do was ask the concierge back at the hotel to book him a table. Without conceit, he knew it wouldn't be a problem once he gave them his name.

'Are you going to be OK or do you want to go back to the hotel?'

Depositing Piers's now crumpled handkerchief on top of her make-up purse in her bag, Emma zipped it shut, put it down by her feet and fervently shook her head. 'I'm fine really. I'm sorry if I embarrassed you in any way.'

'Perhaps you'd like to ring your grandmother when we get back to the hotel? Reassure yourself that she's safe and well.'

'Yes, I'll do that. Thank you.'

Silence descended upon them. Emma found herself wishing she could read the incomprehensible expression crossing Piers's arrestingly attractive face. Had he decided it was a waste of time pursuing this particular liaison after all?

'Here comes the rain.'

His comment had her glancing disconsolately out at the previously sunny street, where a grey cloud had strategically anchored itself overhead and light but steady drops of rain had now started to fall. For a moment or two she watched people quicken their steps and one or two dash into another nearby café for cover, her heart desolate because she seemed destined to disappoint this man. Was it too late to try and make amends, to make him realise that she was still as attracted to him as ever?

'Perhaps you'd tell me a little about your work—what exactly is it that you do?'

Talking about work was the last thing Piers wanted to do, but Emma was gazing at him with such a determined 'I'm going to make conversation if it kills me' look in her sweet brown eyes that he could hardly refuse.

'I'm chief of one of the world's leading management consulting firms. Our main focus is helping clients achieve their financial aspirations. I could go into more detail but quite frankly I wouldn't be a very good host if I bored you to death, so let's talk about something else instead, shall we?'

'Why do you think I'd be bored? Do you think just because I'm a waitress I wouldn't be intelligent enough to understand you?'

'No.' The offence in her tone momentarily took Piers aback. 'I don't think that at all.' Taking a sip of the aromatic coffee in his cup, he drummed his fingers restlessly on the table with his free hand. The previous warmth in his blue eyes had cooled to a light frost when he next trained them on Emma. 'Some men might need to bolster their egos by impressing their dates with what they do for a living, but you see, Emma, my job is something I do— it's not who I am. That's why I don't particularly want to talk about it. It has nothing to do with your profession.'

Even though he sounded irritated, his words still managed to reassure Emma. She wasn't usually so sensitive about her job but it was very easy to fall into that trap with someone as successful and powerful as the man who sat opposite her. Yet, strangely, she felt an unexpected kinship with Piers now because she guessed he must get pretty peeved with people who couldn't see past his job, illustrious as it was, to the man underneath. Contrary to what he might imagine, she for one would love to know the real Piers Redfield. But right now the barriers had come up, and Emma wondered if she'd blown her chances completely.

'We live in a very acquisitive society,' she said. 'Nowadays people are judged more than ever by what they have, where they live, what job they do. You get to meet people from all walks of life when you do a job like mine and you can often tell by their attitudes what their knee-jerk judgements about you are.'

Her surprising comment made Piers sit up straight in his chair. Emma was a beautiful, intelligent woman and he knew he was about to make the same 'knee-jerk' judgement, but what *was* she doing working as a waitress when she was clearly capable of so much more?

'Doesn't that bother you?' he asked.

Her smooth brows drew together. 'Of course it does! What people don't see is that sometimes one's personal circumstances make it difficult to make a different choice. It makes me furious that people would be so arrogant as to judge me. Sometimes it hurts too…especially on days when I'm not exactly feeling my best. On days like those I usually go home and pour out my heart to Lawrence. He has his mood swings but he's a good listener. If he was having a bad day too we'd make popcorn, sit on his sofa or mine and watch a movie to take our minds off things.'

Taken aback by this unexpected insight into his son's life, Piers didn't know what to say. It was far easier to dismiss Lawrence as a waste of space when he didn't know the minutiae of his day-to-day existence—the things that made him into a real person. For a moment Piers was stung by the realisation that there had been very little effort on his part to bridge the unhappy gap between himself and his son. Up until now all he'd done was judge him and blame him. But thinking about Lawrence curled up on a sofa with Emma stung him even more. In fact, it made him completely lose his appetite for the sweet, sticky pastry sitting on the plate in front of him.

'I take it you're going to miss him when he goes down to Cornwall, then…despite the fact you two fell out.' Once more Piers drummed his fingers on the table with its green and white checked cloth and Emma saw the tension bracketing his mouth.

'Actually, we did get the opportunity to make up. I'm

glad, because I could never be really angry with Lawrence for long.'

Piers said nothing. Gazing at the now teeming rain that splattered against the pavement, he wondered if he'd made a mistake in persuading Emma to come with him to Paris. Had she told him the real truth about herself and Lawrence? If her feelings for his son ran deeper than she was letting on, he had no right to circumvent them by coercing her into a sexual relationship with him. But it was so hard not to want the beautiful girl sitting opposite him in the most carnal way and Piers was no celibate monk. Just being with her heightened all his senses almost unbearably. Right now he was acutely sensitive to every little flutter of her exquisite eyelashes, let alone what it did to him when she inadvertently wetted her lips with her tongue or sighed. Now, as she turned her lustrous brown eyes towards him, her gaze clearly troubled, Piers knew it would take a better man than him not to follow through with his desire to seduce her.

'Why don't we drink up our coffee and go back to the hotel?'

'But we've not long left. I thought we were going to take a walk and see some of the sights.'

'We can do that afterwards.'

'After what?'

'Some things are more easily explained when we're on our own.' Pushing back his chair, Piers strode around to where Emma sat, dragged her up to his chest then kissed her openly on the mouth in full view of all the other diners. In his mind he made no apology for deliberately using all his powers of seduction to coax her response and his satisfaction was primordial and savage when he sensed her start to melt.

'That's why,' he said, his breathing harsh as he glanced down into her startled face.

Stunned by the bold, naked need that burned in his eyes, Emma felt her heart flutter with all the wildness of a caged animal who'd suddenly found the cage door left open, and dazedly extricated herself from his embrace to somehow pick up her bag. When she straightened again, Piers was signalling the waiter, his impatience clear as he retrieved his wallet and took out some notes to pay the bill. As they prepared to go out into the rain, Emma silently assured herself that of course she could walk on limbs that seemed as insubstantial as the wire and papier mâché that Lawrence used to fashion his puzzling sculptures.

Paris was as charming in the rain as it was in the sunshine, but Emma paid scant attention to the elegant architecture of the buildings and bright shop-fronts as, with her hand in Piers's, they splashed through puddles and ducked down narrow little alleyways to hurry back to their hotel. Excitement and desire had suppressed any lingering awkwardness in an erotic haze of heat, and by the time they were in the elevator going up to their suite it was impossible for them to take their eyes off each other. Without a doubt, Emma knew that if the elderly lady with the netted veil on her black hat hadn't travelled up with them, thereby curtailing their lust, she and Piers would have been plastered to each other as closely as the rain had plastered their hair to their heads. As it was, Emma was trembling almost uncontrollably as Piers opened the door to their suite and, with his hand at her back, urged her inside with all the urgency of a man on a mission.

The damp, sleek darkness of her soft brown hair brought her delightfully arranged features into stark relief and her skin appeared as clean and as pure as rain-washed crystal as Piers simply stood and appreciated every inch of her loveliness. Inadvertently licking her lips, Emma let a soft sigh escape her as her shimmering dark gaze discovered a sudden helpless fascination for his mouth and the sound was like the whisper of feathers across Piers's already heightened senses. Shrugging off his jacket he heedlessly let it fall to the floor, driven now by a need so powerful that he hardly knew how to contain it.

'Let's get you out of those wet clothes,' he said gruffly, his hands already on the buttons of her coat, popping each one with chilled, urgent fingers. When he'd discarded her outer clothing, he anchored his hands around the hem of her black sweater and, before Emma could utter a word, he lifted it over her head and threw it carelessly to one side to join their coats on the floor. The ache in his groin driving him on, Piers's hungry gaze swept with full red-blooded male gratitude across Emma's sexy curves, then, anchoring his hands firmly on her hips, impelled her hard against his body as his mouth came down to hotly mate with hers.

The bristles on his jaw scraped her tender skin but Emma didn't care, not when his passionate onslaught was the most divine thing she'd ever experienced and the hard, demanding evidence of his desire was pressing into her pelvis ever more urgently. Now it was her turn to tug at his sweater, her senses thrumming in eager anticipation as he helped her to remove it. When Piers's broad, hard-muscled chest was bare, he urged Emma down onto the thick, luxurious carpet—both of them too caught up in the moment to think about moving as far as the bedroom. Removing her shoes, he expertly worked her hosiery down her legs, then did the same with her pink silk and lace panties. When he would have removed her skirt too, Emma held on to it for modesty's sake, suddenly shy in front of those penetrating blue eyes. Her damp hair drifting into

her eyes, her whole body shivering with need, she felt the
door behind her shoulders and leant back against it with
relief because her limbs felt almost too weak to support
her.

As Piers slid his hands sensually up her thighs—ever
closer to the place she longed to feel his touch the most—
Emma's breath was released in a hot little rush, her heart
pounding in delicious anticipation inside her chest. Finding
her warm, soft centre, he slid long, strong fingers inside
her, at the same time kissing each breast in turn through
the insubstantial lace of her bra, nipping and playing with
each tightly puckered nipple until Emma thought the pure,
almost unbearable pleasure this provoked would drive her
insane.

'Piers… Oh, Piers!' His name came out on a husky,
broken croak as he widened her with his clever, stroking
fingers and Emma registered the languorous, drenching
heat at her core with a delicious little quiver of shock.
Then she was grabbing on to him, anchoring her hands on
the powerful banks of his shoulders as, with a knowing
little smile, he withdrew to ease down the zipper on his
jeans. Fascinated by the primitive manifestation of his desire, Emma couldn't suppress a little shudder of fear as she
thought of taking him inside her. Even though she longed
for his possession with every aching, throbbing cell in her
body, it had been a long time since she'd had a lover and
she hoped she would be able to pleasure him as much as
she instinctively knew he would pleasure her.

But there was no time to voice her fears as Piers urged
her to lie down on the carpet, his knee urging her trembling
thighs apart, then, with one deep, sure stroke, plunged inside her and grew suddenly still. Emma couldn't hear herself think over the frighteningly loud thump of her heart.
As she met Piers's rapaciously possessive stare, his eyes

and his touch seemed to brand her. He made her feel altogether wild—like a girl who'd laugh in the face of caution instead of being manacled by her fears. Her apprehension had proved to be quite unfounded. He filled and completed her as if he was that lost part of herself that she'd been secretly hoping to find again one day, but had almost given up hope. As he began to move inside her, lowering his head to claim her mouth in a long, melting kiss, drugging her with his lips, his tongue, his deeply sensual heat, Emma knew that every passionate moment was being imprinted on her heart and mind forever.

Gazing at the stunningly lovely girl beneath him, her dark hair, her bewitching eyes, her ripe, womanly breasts, Piers knew right then that he was the luckiest man in the universe. As her damp, scalding heat wrapped around his manhood his pleasure multiplied, his mind and body enslaved by the erotic heat that threatened to grow into a conflagration, and he couldn't remember another time when sex had felt so good…so right. As Emma instinctively raised her hips to accommodate his ever more powerful thrusts, Piers felt the tension inside him escalate quickly to the point of no return. Sensing that she too was almost at that point, he kissed her breasts, settled on one and drew it deeply into his mouth, his teeth freeing the tight, dusky peak from its pink lace enclosure, registering her buck beneath him, then her muscles closing tightly around him. Again and again they convulsed until Piers wanted to howl with the ecstasy of it.

'I can't stop… Oh, Piers.' There didn't seem to be any way that Emma could prevent the tears that gathered at the corners of her eyes and spilled hotly down her cheeks. As she reached the peak of sensation it had swept through her like a cyclone, ripping away every secret she'd ever had and leaving her emotions helplessly bared to the man who had taken her there.

Desperately seeking her moist, ravished mouth, Piers kissed her one more time before she realised that for him too there was no going back. The harsh groan that ripped from his lips as he glanced up finally made Emma realise the enormity of what had just occurred between them. They'd been so crazy for each other that neither had stopped to think about protection. She could hardly believe she was capable of such irresponsible insanity.

'You are utterly beautiful in every way.' The sheer intensity of Piers's heated gaze momentarily stilled her fears and when he smoothed Emma's still damp hair away from her forehead and placed his lips there almost reverently, she knew irrevocably that she'd never be able to walk away from this man with her heart and soul intact. He had branded her, and she'd willingly let him.

'Stay there,' he instructed now, pulling on his silk boxers and zipping up his trousers. Back only moments later with a generous white bathrobe, Piers helped Emma into it as tenderly as if she were a child, fastening the towelling belt with an extra little tug and a sexy little smile that made her limbs turn to jelly. He was alternately passionate and tender, and Emma had no defence against such skilful seduction.

'Do you want to come to bed or would you rather take a bath?'

'A bath?' Torn between wanting to prolong their lovemaking and soaking in hot, scented water in a beautifully appointed bathtub complete with gold taps and enough perfumes and bath oil to stock a chemist, Emma chewed down guiltily on her soft lower lip.

'I meant a bath with me,' Piers said gruffly, then lifted

her off her feet and swung her expertly into his arms as though she were as light as air.

'Oh!'

'I hope you're going to have a lot more to say for yourself than that by the time I've finished with you, young lady.' Chuckling, he headed for the stunning marble bathroom with all the confidence of a man who'd made the conquest he'd long been craving, and couldn't help wondering how many more times he'd have to make love to Emma before he could truly call himself satisfied.

Later at dinner, wearing the gorgeous little black dress with its dipping beaded neckline that Fleur had surprised her with, Emma glanced around her at the other elegantly attired patrons of the exclusive but discreet little restaurant, and consciously committed every little detail to memory. It would sustain her during the no doubt tense days ahead when her grandmother was in hospital and afterwards— when she returned home to recuperate, and when Emma would be even more devoted to her care. But more than the place, the dress or the seemingly endless array of beauty and elegance that epitomised this fascinating city, she would remember the man who'd brought her here. Now, as Piers glanced at her with that confident, knowing little smile of his that turned her insides to butter, Emma recalled the excitement of their lovemaking and felt a fierce little spurt of heat coil in her stomach and spread down between her thighs. It was amazing how much more pleasurable bathing was when it was shared with a man as inventive and as passionate as Piers… Blushing profusely at the thought, Emma rubbed at the sudden chill on her bare arms and dared a glance back.

'Will you go down to Cornwall to visit Lawrence once he's settled?'

The question was out before she could check it and she guessed it must have been preying on her mind. Piers's smile immediately vanished. 'I don't know. It depends on whether or not I'd be welcome.'

Progress! At least he hadn't said he wouldn't consider it. Emma felt a flare of hope. It wasn't right that father and son should be so disunited—not when, to her mind, they clearly needed each other more than either of them was admitting. She knew Piers was a busy man in constant demand because of the responsibilities of his chosen career—but work shouldn't always be the top priority in his life, should it? At the end of the day it was people who mattered and none should matter more than one's own children.

'I'm sure he'd be thrilled to see you.'

'Perhaps ''thrilled'' is overstating the case just a little, don't you think?'

'I know Lawrence can be a little rash and unthinking in what he says sometimes, but I really believe underneath all that outward bluff is a very caring and sometimes lonely young man.'

Lonely he might be prepared to believe…but caring? All the evidence made him beg him to differ. Feeling the tension knotting his stomach muscles, Piers breathed out slowly to try and release it.

'It seems almost impossible for you to see the less than ideal in anyone.' Reaching for her hand, Piers turned it over in his palm to examine it, thinking how small and delicate her fingers were—how perfect.

'What's wrong with that?'

'You wouldn't survive two minutes in the corporate world, sweetheart.'

'Then it's a good job I'm just a plain old waitress, isn't it?' Secretly elated at the small endearment he'd addressed her with, Emma carefully extricated her hand, already anxious that she might be getting a little more used to his touch than was good for her.

'Never plain, and quite frankly I wouldn't want you to be a part of that world for even a second. Much better to view the world with rose-tinted glasses for as long as you can and be the best waitress on the planet than be so driven by ambition that you'd trample over your own mother to get to the top.' It surprised Piers how vehemently he meant that, but after spending the entire afternoon introducing his beautiful young lover to the joys of lovemaking, he realised she was definitely bringing out his protective streak.

Particularly so because now there was a distinct possibility that he'd made her pregnant. He'd only been reckless that very first time and afterwards he'd been more sensible and used protection, but he had still taken a risk he should never have taken. Accepting that he was the one who should have known better, Piers laid none of the blame at Emma's door. He had been so dazed by his lust for her—his only goal to make her his—that he'd left his ability to think back at the café where they'd been having coffee. Whatever happened he would take care of it. And he had to let her know that.

'Emma, I could have made you pregnant…unless, of course, you're on the Pill. Are you?' His glance intensified as he saw hot, embarrassed colour pour into Emma's cheeks. She touched her white napkin to her lips for a moment as if to compose herself, and Piers didn't miss the fact that her hand was shaking slightly as she laid it back down on the table.

'No, I'm not on the Pill. I'm allergic to that kind of contraception. Besides…there was no need for me to be. It's been a long time since I've…I mean, since I had someone in my life.'

Piers couldn't deny the swift stab of satisfaction that throbbed through him at her words—even though, realistically speaking, he knew their association wasn't destined to be a long one. After this weekend, he couldn't promise that he would see her again soon. Firstly he had a busy schedule ahead of him that involved at least three months of foreign travel, and secondly Emma had said herself that she had commitments—her sick grandmother being one. Unless it transpired in the course of events that Emma was pregnant, the kindest thing to do would be to kiss her goodbye at Heathrow Airport tomorrow on their return and let her go for good. Selfishly speaking, Piers honestly hoped she wasn't pregnant. He had already failed spectacularly the first time around as a father and he had no desire whatsoever to repeat the experience.

'If the worse comes to the worst I don't want you to worry, Emma. Obviously we're unlikely to see each other again after this weekend, but I'm a wealthy man and whatever you decide to do I will naturally support you financially.'

CHAPTER EIGHT

FEELING as if she was plunging over the side of a mountain, Emma stared at Piers in utter disbelief. In a few short, heartless words he had coldly reminded her that their association had come about for one reason and one reason only, and now that he'd had what he wanted all along he could dispense with her services forthwith. Oh, he would take care of any less than perfect elements of their little liaison—like Emma winding up pregnant—but paying her off was probably a small price to pay to get her out of his hair. Well…at least after they left the hotel. Anger, hurt and shame rained down on her with all the drowning force of a deluge and Emma sat there trembling, almost too upset to even speak.

'If the worst comes to the worst?'

'Let's be realistic, Emma. Don't pretend you could possibly be happy about it if you did find out you were pregnant.'

Flinching at the disdain in his voice, Emma didn't know how she managed to stay seated. 'How do you know that? You don't even know me!'

'Children change your life forever. You're only twenty-five, Emma. What life have you seen yet? Don't you want to travel? Meet people? Expand your horizons in some way? If you had a child all those ambitions would go on the back burner for a long time.'

'There speaks the voice of experience, I suppose. What's the matter, Piers, did having Lawrence cramp your style? I don't suppose you wanted to be a father at all, did you? Is that why you resent him so much?' Emma's heart was beating too hard and too fast but it was too late now to take her angry words back. He had hurt her with his scornful assumptions about whether or not she should welcome the possibility of having a child and she had hit back using the one weapon that would get to him the most— his son.

A telling muscle ticked briefly in the side of that perfectly cut jaw and all the colour seemed to drain from Piers's face. 'I never said I didn't want to be a father. And whatever may be going on between Lawrence and myself is my business and my business alone, and I'll thank you to keep out of it. My son never *cramped my style,* as you put it. Everything I did, everything I worked for was ultimately for him. The fact that it turns out my being there more often would have been the best thing I could have done for him, and I only saw that too late, is my loss and my everlasting regret…but you can't turn back the clock.'

There was genuine pain behind his words but his careful expression of control scarcely supported it. Even though she sympathised with him, Emma was still undeniably hurt that his only offer of support if she was to fall pregnant with his child would be financial. Clearly he would want nothing to do with her other than that. Yet again, she felt like the heartbroken nine-year-old whose father had walked out the door one day and never came back…

'I have feelings.' The lump in her throat was so painful that Emma could hardly get the words out. Fighting back tears, she glanced directly at Piers. In the candlelight that burned between them on the table, the shadows and planes that made up his extraordinary face were even more compelling. In the expensive Italian suit that was a deserved compliment to his strong, impressive physique, he exuded sophistication and wealth with an ease that was enviable.

And it just served to point up the vast differences between him and Emma even more. But the most intimidating thing of all was that, behind that mask of handsome sophistication, his emotions were so skilfully hidden she'd have to be a magician to locate them. It was that realisation that disturbed Emma the most. She could reveal any number of things to him that were in her heart, especially the fact that she needed to be needed and felt unwanted and useless when she wasn't. She could tell him that when it came to helping her friends she'd walk over hot coals, but when it came to helping herself she simply lacked the courage or the self-belief that was required. She could explain all that to Piers and he would still regard her with that detached, superior air that made her feel anything but his equal. The only interest he had in a girl like her was sexual. It was as base and demoralising as that, and the only reason she was sitting here in this exclusive Parisian restaurant. She would do well to remember it.

'What feelings, Emma?'

'That's just it.' Staring down at the beautifully presented meal on her plate, Emma linked her hands in her lap then captured her fingers tightly in a bid to stop their trembling. 'You're not interested in feelings, are you, Piers? You wanted a nice, uncomplicated dirty weekend and what you got instead was me.'

His blue eyes turned ominously dark. 'Don't talk like that!'

'Why not? Because you don't like hearing the truth? Would you prefer it if I dressed it up with polite little phrases that disguise what's really going on?'

'So tell me.' His jaw clenched tight, his eyes flashed a warning that Emma refused to heed. 'What's *really* going on, Emma?'

Her face burning, Emma couldn't hold back the tide of

emotion that threatened to submerge her. 'I know I'm not the usual kind of woman you take out. I don't know why you singled me out… Perhaps you wanted to try something new. A twenty-five-year-old waitress must certainly be a novelty to a man in your position. Perhaps you thought I'd be grateful you even glanced my way. When it comes right down to it, all you wanted was a girl for the weekend. What you didn't want was someone who had feelings… Someone who might not feel so good about being used by a man who is so used to getting what he wants that he's hardly going to notice if she demonstrates the slightest reservation.'

'As far as I'm aware I never *used* you, Emma. We had consensual sex, remember? Sorry if it hurts, sweetheart, but I didn't hear any protests from you at the time.'

His words ripped into her tender flesh like a hot blade. 'You know what? When you came looking for me at the restaurant I should have just told you to go to hell!' Throwing down her napkin on the table, her whole body quaking with rage, Emma pushed to her feet, collected her evening bag and escaped in the direction of the ladies' restroom before Piers knew what had hit him.

Five minutes later when she emerged Emma asked one of the waitresses to fetch her coat, slipped it on, then stepped out into the rainy Parisian night without even the faintest idea of where she would go. All she knew was that right now Piers Redfield was the last person in the world she wanted to be with. Up until a short while ago he'd been kind and considerate, the perfect gentleman in every way…but as soon as he thought that he might have made her pregnant, his attitude had changed completely.

But how stupid of her to even imagine for one second that it wouldn't. He was Piers Redfield, corporate wizard, millionaire high flyer, and his world and Emma's were so far apart that you could fit an entire galaxy between them. The last thing he wanted was to get some tiresome little waitress pregnant and have her make life difficult for him! But it was hardly Piers's fault that Emma had been so mesmerised by him that she'd managed to almost forget who he was for a day. Up until a little while ago they'd been just like any other pair of lovers in the most romantic city in the world, but now Emma had come back down to earth with an almighty crash. Slowing her pace because her legs were shaking so badly, she pulled up the collar on her camel-coloured coat then set her face determinedly towards the route that led along the left bank of the Seine. She didn't care where it led her—she only knew that it didn't matter as long as it was miles away from Piers.

He knew the possibility of finding her in the busy night-time streets of the city were slim to nothing, but that didn't stop Piers from walking for nearly two hours straight in the hope that Emma might show up. Of course he had rung the hotel several times on his mobile phone as he walked, regularly checking in with Reception in case she decided to go back there, even though in his heart of hearts he knew she most likely wouldn't.

And who could blame her? His intentions might have been honourable, in trying to reassure her about supporting her financially should she fall pregnant, but at the end of the day all he'd done was make her furious with him. So furious that she'd walked off without telling him where she was going—and, more worryingly, was now alone in a strange city.

Finally, when teeming rain had driven him back to the hotel in search of shelter and dry clothes, Piers ordered a brandy at the bar then sat broodingly staring into his glass, from time to time glancing at his watch, his nerves stretched taut as a guitar string. Inwardly, he cursed himself for handling the whole situation with all the tact and finesse of a herd of wildebeest. Emma was just an innocent young girl who'd befriended his son, working hard to make ends meet, worrying about her sick grandmother, putting everybody else's needs ahead of her own as far as Piers could deduce. Highly commendable qualities that would make any man desire and admire her as a woman even more. But those very qualities in Emma just pointed up the fact that when it came to caring for others, Piers was definitely wanting in that department. And he had used her. Emma was right. Whatever way he looked at it, he couldn't make his motives sound any prettier. He'd seen her and desired her, then relentlessly pursued her in the hope of gratifying his lust and—worse than that—getting one over on Lawrence. The fact that she'd been a willing partner in their lovemaking didn't absolve him of the fact that he had been the driving force in their association. Not for one moment had he stopped to consider the effect that association would have on Emma or how it would impact on her life.

Now he just longed for her to walk back into the hotel and at least give him the chance to make amends. He might not be able to offer her much more than a nice time but he was sincere in his concern for her welfare. Despite what she'd said, she could hardly welcome the idea of becoming a single mother and Piers had to be realistic even if she refused to be. Even waitresses in the top eateries didn't earn a fortune, and he hated the idea that Emma would struggle to raise a child without financial help from him. Oh, lord…if only he hadn't been so crazy for her he might have thought about the necessity for protection from the beginning. But hindsight was a wonderful thing and didn't allow for surprises like passion so blazing hot that it made you forget your own name never mind having safe sex.

Taking a generous slug of brandy, Piers welcomed the burning trail down his throat to his stomach. Whatever happened, he told himself, it was academic because he probably wouldn't even see her again after this weekend. It just wasn't on the cards when on his return to the UK he was going to leave the country for nigh on three months.

A hand touched him on the shoulder and Piers almost leapt out of his seat in shock. An apologetic staff member explained to him that they had just received a message from Mademoiselle Robards that said she was spending the night with a girlfriend and would return to the hotel in the morning.

After relief had washed over him that she was safe, Piers couldn't deny the shattering disappointment that welled up inside his chest at the thought of not seeing Emma until the morning. All of a sudden he was consumed with the need to make up with her, to hold her in his arms and show her in every conceivable way just how sorry he was he'd upset her. Unable to do that and unreasonably angry that she hadn't thought to furnish him with her friend's address or telephone number, Piers turned back to the ever solicitous barman and ordered another brandy.

Before returning to the hotel the next morning, Emma spent over two hours visiting Notre Dame Cathedral, her hurt and unhappiness for a moment put aside as she wandered around inside the vast, awe-inspiring edifice. The light that illuminated the interior came purely from hundreds upon hundreds of glowing candles and the sight was utterly breathtaking. Finding herself alone in one of the several small chapels, Emma lit a candle, said a prayer for her grandmother's return to health, then spent several tortured minutes anguishing about her growing feelings for Piers. In spite of her outburst last night at the restaurant, she was still mesmerised by the man. It was her own fault, Emma scolded herself. She should have been stronger where he was concerned. She should never have agreed to come to Paris with him…and, most of all, she should never have allowed him to seduce her so recklessly that she hadn't even given a thought to protecting herself from the possible consequences.

Fleur had insisted Emma was being much too hard on herself. Her friend seemed to believe that somehow Piers would see that he was in the wrong, that of course he would want to see Emma again after this weekend—why shouldn't he? Emma was a beautiful young girl and he should count his blessings! She just hadn't been able to get it through to Fleur that Piers was an important man: he wasn't going to waste his time with a girl like Emma when he could take his pick where women were concerned. And beautiful, sophisticated women from his own eminent stratosphere, at that.

'My job is not who I am…' Why did that particular comment come back just then to taunt her and fill her with longing? *Because you're a fool, Emma Robards, that's why!* Turning away from myriad glowing candles, Emma hurried from the peaceful haven of the little chapel with its heart-rending images of the Madonna and child and the drugging, sweet-smelling incense that pervaded the air, suddenly desperate to be outside again. Then, the thought filling her with equal doses of dread and hope, she decided to go back to the hotel, where no doubt Piers would be waiting—probably with her suitcases packed, and ready to deposit her back to the airport.

*   *   *

'Have you had breakfast?' Was it his imagination or had his heart suddenly galloped in his chest at the sight of her? There was certainly a multitude of strong emotions vying for precedence as he allowed his starved gaze to wander from the top of Emma's glossy brown hair to the tips of her feet in her delicate little open-toed sandals. Had she walked the streets of Paris in those shoes? Recalling her obvious discomfort in high heels, Piers was about to suggest she discard them and go barefoot when, as if reading his mind, she bent down to release the narrow black straps around her ankles and kicked off her shoes with a sigh. When she stood up her cheeks were pink and her eyes wary, her glance nervously breaking away to wander around the room; she was looking anywhere, it seemed, rather than look at Piers.

'I had croissants and coffee with Fleur before she left to go and see her boyfriend.' Undoing the buttons of her coat, she slipped her fingers through her long chestnut hair then let it fall softly again around her face.

'I was very concerned when you took off like that last night. It was reckless behaviour, Emma—anything could have happened!'

So he was 'concerned' but not sorry? Her throat constricting unhappily, Emma couldn't prevent her snort of derision. 'You're probably just angry because I inconvenienced you—not because you give a damn! Be honest, Piers—all that concerns you now is that I might be pregnant. But don't worry, because no matter what happens you're the last person in the world I'd come to for help, so you can breathe easy. I promise when we return to London this evening, you won't see or hear of me again!'

Determinedly on her way to the bedroom to pack her case, Emma squealed in shock when Piers grabbed hold of her arm and swung her around to face him. His eyes were dazzlingly blue and spitting fire and for a moment she was light-headed with fear.

'What makes you so damn sure I don't want to see you again?' he demanded savagely. Barely registering the question, Emma slid her gaze as if spellbound down to his mouth—that perfectly designed instrument of delight that made her curl her toes just looking at it, especially when she vividly recalled that practically every inch of her body knew the innate mastery of its touch so intimately...

'Oh, please don't insult me by telling me you've had a change of heart! Or is it that you just thought you'd get your money's worth before the weekend is up?' Wrenching her arm free, Emma barely had a moment to think before she found herself crushed up against the adamantine wall of Piers's chest, her anger suddenly quelled by the shocking feelings of submission and desire washing through her. Feelings engendered by the captivating textures of the hard male body that was pressing so relentlessly against her own softer curves. Her legs started to shake, growing feebly weak as she struggled to stay in control.

'Don't pretend you don't desire me as much as I desire you.' His face was very close. So close that every dark blond eyelash and every lightly grooved line spreading outward from his incredibly compelling eyes was revealed in stunning clarity. Up close, they were devastating. Her stomach dropped to her shoes. Oh, God! What were they doing? She didn't want them to waste precious time fighting. Even though there was probably not so much as an ounce of hope for their shared future, something urged her to make the most of these short-lived moments together because Emma wasn't sure that there ever would or could be another man she was so wildly attracted to again...

'I didn't say I didn't desire you.' Her lip quivering, her

eyes were dark and shimmering as she gazed up into Piers's. 'But I have feelings…even if you don't. Your offer of help was so—so clinical. I know you're probably used to dealing with problems extremely efficiently, but I don't want to be seen as some kind of problem that has to be dealt with then conveniently forgotten! I'm a human being, Piers. Granted, I'm maybe not as sophisticated as some of your girlfriends who can easily accept that all you want is the physical—and some casual fling at that—but that doesn't mean I'm any less deserving of your respect.'

'I do respect you, damn it!'

Because at that moment he was torn between kissing her and shaking her, Piers let her go and walked away. Emma was stirring up feelings inside him that he expressly didn't welcome. Feelings didn't feature largely in his *modus operandi* as a rule. His life was complicated enough without allowing emotions to call the shots. He only had to remember his life with Naomi all those years ago to recall how explosive and dangerous emotions were. He had been devastated when she'd died in a car accident, but after the first couple of years after her death had gone by, he was ashamed to say he'd started to feel relief at the fact she wasn't around. The woman had put him through hell with her affairs, her lying and her constant accusations that he was a cold, callous bastard who didn't care about his family. Piers didn't want that stress again—ever.

They should never have got married so young. But with Lawrence on the way and his sense of responsibility for the nineteen-year-old Naomi kicking in, Piers had not stopped to consider his true feelings for his girlfriend. He'd convinced himself he'd loved her when he really hadn't. After a while Naomi had obviously sensed the fact and sought to pay him back by having as many affairs as she could. Being so young, she hadn't had the maturity to ride out the storm and try and win back her husband's affection in some way. The truth was that they'd both made an almighty mess of things—a mess that had repercussions even to this day, when poor Naomi was no longer around. Piers only had to think of the hostility in his son's blue eyes to be reminded of that.

Striding to the window now, he stood gazing out at the fashionable little courtyard at the back of the hotel where patrons relaxed at wrought-iron tables, sipped coffee and enjoyed easy conversation in the bright winter sunshine. For a fervent few moments he wished that he and Emma could do the same but suddenly somehow—without him expecting it—their relationship had developed into something far more complicated than he'd anticipated. There was nothing easy or simple about their situation anymore. And even though desire was flowing through his veins with all the combined force of storm and flood, Piers knew it would be wrong to tumble into bed with Emma again when it was obvious she was in turmoil about being here with him in the first place.

'It's probably difficult for you to understand the kind of frenetic life I lead unless you've been in it. I'll tell you the truth, Emma—it doesn't make for lasting relationships. My relationships with women are usually brief out of necessity…though I have to say, we usually part as friends.'

'Is that what you want me to be? Your friend?'

No. Having become intimately acquainted with Emma's divine body, there was no way Piers could even think about reverting to a platonic relationship. Even he wasn't *that* strong.

'When we get back to the UK I'm practically flying straight out again to Australia. From there I go on to New Zealand, Indonesia, Bali and then South Africa. I'm going to be away for at least three months. Right now I can't promise you very much except that I will get in touch when I get back.'

Emma's heart sank as if it were weighted down with a heavy stone. It was obvious to her that he was just trying to placate. He hadn't even expressed a desire to have her as a friend, so clearly he had no real intentions of seeing her again at all.

'I understand.' Her fingers curled tightly into her palm. Without Piers saying another word, she knew the subject was now strictly off limits for the rest of their trip and her heart grieved that that was the case.

'So…how about us spending the rest of the day doing some sightseeing together?' Jamming his hands into his trouser pockets, Piers dragged up a smile from somewhere, though right then it was the last thing he felt like doing. What he *could* do was try and make damn sure Emma enjoyed her last day in Paris. Make up for their disastrous dinner date last night, at least.

'Sightseeing?' Emma frowned.

'You know: the Eiffel Tower, the Louvre, Notre Dame?'

'I saw the Eiffel Tower and the Louvre with Miles yesterday, remember? And this morning after I left Fleur's, I went to Notre Dame. I wanted to light a candle for my grandmother.'

Now, why did that last comment make him feel ten times worse? Because she was an angel and he had taken unfair advantage of the fact… Self-loathing rolled through him and he silently cursed it. Sighing, he withdrew his hands from his pockets and grimaced instead.

'Things haven't turned out the way I'd hoped—not by a long shot. Yesterday I had to work and today… Well, anyway, I should have taken you to all those places myself.'

Sensing his genuine regret, Emma couldn't find it in her

heart to refuse him. 'There's still plenty to see, isn't there? I mean…if you'd like to, that is?' She couldn't pretend she hadn't been hoping to make love with Piers one last time. But now everything was changed…spoiled. Looming over them both was the fact that Emma might even now be pregnant. Because of her allergy to oral contraception, she couldn't even take the morning-after pill to circumvent matters. But silently acknowledging that Piers was probably feeling bad enough about the way things had turned out—not least the accusations she had levelled at him— she could hardly find fault with his suggestion that they make things easier for themselves by doing some harmless sightseeing instead.

'Yes, I'd like to. You want to change out of that dress first? As eye-catching as it undoubtedly is, I think you'd be more comfortable in something a bit more casual, don't you?'

Fingering the buttons on her coat, Emma self-consciously pulled the lapels of the garment across the black beaded bodice of her elegant couture dress, acknowledging to herself that it would probably be a long time before she ever had occasion to wear it again. Perhaps never if all it did was conjure up bitter-sweet memories of Piers…

'Miles will drive you home.'

'But what about you?' Standing in the busy mêlée of Heathrow Airport, Emma wished the moment of parting hadn't arrived so soon. Their last afternoon in Paris had come to an end far too quickly and now she was faced with the reality of her homecoming. Sliding a hand into her coat pocket, she glanced down at her luggage, then at Miles a few feet away, standing patiently by the sliding doors marked 'Exit.' She caught his eye for a moment, glimpsing what appeared to be a reassuring smile.

'I'm meeting a colleague at a nearby hotel. Miles will come back for me when he's dropped you off.'

'You're sure?'

Unable to stop himself from touching her, Piers reached out and stroked her cheek with the flat of his hand. Her big eyes looked so anxious and unhappy that he felt an acute pang of sharp regret that he had to let her go. Now it came down to it, he asked himself if he wasn't being too hasty in concluding that a relationship between them could never be. Just the thought of her being in someone else's arms instead of his was agony. But what could he promise her? His lifestyle was so frenetic and disjointed and Emma was hardly equipped to jump from waitress to corporate wife, expected to act as hostess to clients and colleagues at the drop of a hat, and everything else that went with being married to someone in Piers's position.

It took him a full minute to fully realise the dangerous road his thoughts were travelling down. *Marriage?* He clenched his jaw tight and gave himself a mental shake.

'I'm absolutely sure. And you must promise me that you'll get in touch if you need anything. If you ring the office my PA, Fiona, will pass on a message wherever I am. You know what I mean, don't you?'

Resisting the urge to lean into the smooth, warm hand that caressed her cheek, Emma stiffened her shoulders. He meant if she was pregnant. But she would rather die than ask him to support her if she should happen to find herself in that terrifying position.

'I'll be fine. There is just one thing I wanted to ask you before I go.'

Reluctantly Piers withdrew the hand that had been stroking that baby-soft cheek. 'Go ahead.'

Her gaze steady, Emma wondered if he thought she might be going to demand something that would make his life difficult. She couldn't wait to show him that once she left him today he wouldn't set eyes on her again if she could help it. He could forget that their little liaison ever happened—which Emma was certain was his preferred option.

'Make friends with Lawrence. He needs you, even if you think he doesn't.'

Her comment catching him on the raw, Piers glanced down at his watch, suddenly glad that he had a legitimate excuse not to linger. Right now Lawrence was the last person he wanted to think about.

'I'll do my best.' He had been going to kiss her but then decided that if he did he probably wouldn't end up going anywhere he needed to go. Emma made him feel all sorts of unsettling emotions that he normally tried so hard to suppress and the sooner he could find his equilibrium again, the better. 'I'm sorry, Emma, but I've got to run. I'm already twenty minutes behind schedule.'

'Then I won't keep you any longer.' Picking up her bags, Emma made herself smile even though it almost killed her to do so. 'Thanks for taking me to Paris. I'll always remember it.'

As she moved gracefully through the throng of people towards the exit and Miles, Piers wondered why, instead of him feeling relieved, his chest was crowded with an entirely different emotion. One he didn't welcome.

CHAPTER NINE

DROPPING down onto the bench seat outside the ICU where she'd just left her grandmother amid a flurry of doctors and nurses, Emma rubbed hard at her temples in an attempt to force away the fear that was currently crashing through her like Niagara Falls. The smell of disinfectant and disease was making her feel as if she wanted to throw up and she clenched her hands, pleading with herself over and over again to try and stay calm. Oh, God…was her precious grandmother going to die? Just two days ago Emma had endured an awkward and unsatisfactory goodbye at the airport with Piers because of the plainly unfinished business between them. Despondent, she'd returned to work, telling herself there was nothing for it but to face the fact that that was probably the last time she would see him again—ever. Her only consolation in the midst of her unhappiness was that she still had one person in her life who loved her unconditionally, and Emma had thanked her lucky stars. With her beloved grandmother's support, she would cope with whatever fate lay at her door in the future. Now all her hopes and reassurances had been upended like a barrel of apples because the worst thing that could possibly happen had happened. Two hours ago in the midst of the lunchtime rush at the bistro, she'd had a phone call to tell her that her grandmother had suffered a heart attack at her home. Liz had driven a stunned Emma to the hospital, only leaving her a few minutes ago to go in search of some coffee for them both.

Nervously plucking some lint off her black skirt, Emma

tried hard to ward off the battery of fearful thoughts that was currently bombarding her, with little success. Hearing the distinct sound of heels clicking down the hall of the white-painted corridor, she turned her head, rising to her feet as Liz approached, two steaming polystyrene cups of coffee in her hands.

'I put plenty of sugar in yours,' she said kindly, handing one to a white-faced Emma.

'Thanks, Liz.'

'Any news?' Glancing anxiously towards the ominously closed grey swing doors, Liz took a wary sip of her scalding beverage.

'Not yet.' Her gaze sliding away from the concern in her friend's eyes, Emma wished she didn't feel so damn helpless. Just a few feet away, the person she cared about most in the whole world was fighting for her life and there was nothing her granddaughter could do except pray.

'Helen is strong,' Liz was assuring her. 'If anyone can pull through it's your grandmother.'

'She shouldn't have had to wait so long for her operation. If I could have afforded for her to be treated privately I would have.'

'I can see where this is heading.' Shaking her head, Liz caught hold of Emma's wrist with her free hand. 'You don't need yet another thing to blame yourself for! All you've done is love and support your gran above and beyond the call of duty, if you want my opinion. I don't know many girls your age who would willingly give up weekend after weekend for the last five years to go and take care of an ailing relative. The last thing that brave lady in there would want is you giving yourself a hard time because you haven't done enough!'

Her lip trembling, Emma bit back the urge to break down and cry. If she recovered from this awful event,

Helen Robards was going to need her even more. Therefore, Emma needed to stay strong. What use would she be to anybody if she was to show weakness now? She didn't remember a lot about her father from her childhood but she did remember him yelling at her mother that he despised her for being so weak. Well, Emma wasn't like her mother. She was made of sterner stuff…wasn't she? No man was going to ever accuse her of depending on him too much. For starters she wasn't going to give them the chance. Least of all Piers Redfield, with his clinical offer to support her financially should she find herself pregnant…

'I had so many plans for her little house. I'd already bought the paint and stuff to do it up while she was in hospital.' Her honey-brown gaze glistening, Emma pulled away from Liz's kind grip on her wrist. As she glanced up and down the clinical corridor with its shabby medical notices on the walls and the wilting potted plants on the stark white sills, fear welled up inside her and wouldn't be tamped. What was she going to do if her grandmother didn't pull through? When Helen Robards went, Emma would have nobody…

Someone pushed open the swing doors. As both women whirled around to see who it was, the middle-aged Chinese surgeon, who had briefly introduced himself to Emma as Mr Lau just after her grandmother had been admitted, stepped forward to talk to her. Although his kind face was carefully blank, Emma couldn't stop herself from fearing the worst.

'I am very sorry, Miss Robards, but your grandmother passed away five minutes ago. Her heart was very weak and unfortunately we could not save her.'

Emma didn't hear anything much after that except the loud rush of blood in her ears. Through numbed lips she thanked the surgeon for doing all he could then shook his hand and allowed Liz to guide her back down onto the bench seat. Her hand trembling, she raised her coffee to her lips and took a sip.

'Would you mind waiting here for a little while? I will send a nurse to come and talk to you. There are things you will need to attend to.'

Looking up, Emma nodded blankly. 'What? Yes…thank you.'

'I'll stay with her,' Liz assured him before watching him march purposefully back through the dark grey doors. Privately she thought he must be relieved that Emma didn't break down in front of him or become upset. God forbid that we should display our humanity and become emotional! Swallowing down her anger at the unfairness of it all, Liz turned back to Emma, sliding her hand behind the younger woman's ramrod-straight back and rubbing it. 'Oh, Emma, I'm so sorry, my love. Of all the terrible things to happen.'

'I'm all right, Liz.' Thankful for the blessed numbness that was currently gripping her, Emma smiled listlessly at her friend. 'Don't worry about me, I'm going to be fine. Honestly.'

'Of course you are…but not yet, hmm? You're allowed to cry, Emma. Don't hold it all inside, please.'

'I don't have time to cry! There are things I need to do.' Pushing herself to her feet, an agitated Emma began to pace the corridor, her low heels echoing down the hall as she walked. 'As soon as that nurse gets here I'm going to make a list.'

Remaining seated, Liz gave a sigh full of sadness for her friend's plight. 'You do whatever you feel you have to, love. And when you're ready to talk…I'll be right here.'

*   *   *

'I insist that you come upstairs and have something to eat with me. You've been walking around like a wraith for the past three days now and I won't have it!'

How like his father he was when he was angry, Emma reflected with a jolt as she glanced up into Lawrence's reproachful blue eyes. And how naturally it came to him to issue orders! Moving away from the door, she glanced disconsolately across the room at the pile of ironing she'd left on the sofa to tackle that evening, knowing that if she didn't do something about it soon she'd be walking around looking like a bag lady. Not that she gave a damn. It was hard to care about anything much since her grandmother had gone but thank God the funeral was over and done with. She'd just about held it together to get through that nightmare but the effort had cost her dearly. Now she was spent and shaken, exhausted by grief, depleted by lack of both sleep and food, and she knew she must look a sight— yet she was still overwhelmingly touched by Lawrence's concern for her well-being.

'I've got too much to do, Lawrence, but thanks all the same.'

'What have you eaten today?' Following her into the room, his worried glance took in the piles of strewn clothing on the sofa, the mug of cold, congealed coffee on the floor and the collection of envelopes and letters spread haphazardly across the coffee-table.

'What have I eaten?' Pressing her fingers against her temples, Emma tried to think. 'I had some cornflakes for breakfast and some toast…or was that yesterday? I really can't remember.' Picking up a blouse from the sofa, she held it up to the light to examine it. There was no way she could avoid ironing it. If there was one thing she prided herself on it was looking good at work.

'Leave it.'

'What?'

'Leave the damn shirt!' Snatching it from her hands, Lawrence threw the offending item back on the sofa. 'If you don't eat you're going to get ill, and if you get ill, how are you going to support yourself, eh?'

He had a point, Emma admitted silently. She'd already lost her grandmother, and it went without saying her relationship with Piers was a lost cause. The last thing she needed to do now was lose her job, although in her heart of hearts she knew she would get nothing but help in that quarter from Adam and Liz. They had both attended the funeral with her and insisted that she take as much time off as she needed—her job would still be waiting for her even if that was six months later. They were good, dear friends, but even though the restaurant was undoubtedly successful they couldn't afford to pay her indefinitely if she wasn't working.

'I can't expect you to cook for me when you're in the middle of packing.' Her brown eyes serious, Emma released a small, defeated sigh. Now it had come to it, she didn't want Lawrence to go. As testing as he could be sometimes, she was genuinely fond of him. Without him the house was going to be far too quiet. At least until a new tenant moved in. She just prayed she wouldn't get some neighbour from hell to top it all off.

'Who said anything about cooking?' With a flash of seriously white teeth, Lawrence grinned shamelessly. 'They don't call me the take-away king for nothing, you know!'

So that was how Emma ended up sitting cross-legged on Lawrence's one remaining rug that hadn't been packed away, eating Chinese food with a can of lemonade and a Rolling Stones accompaniment on the stereo. All around them were packing cases and tea chests crammed full of Lawrence's belongings and the dull grape-coloured walls were stripped bare of all the colourful artwork that he had created and hung there for almost a year now. The place just wouldn't be the same without him, Emma thought sadly, spearing some beanshoots onto her fork.

'So…you didn't tell me. How was Paris?'

His question, coming out of nowhere, made her drop her fork back onto the plate with a clatter.

'How did you know I went to Paris?' Dry-mouthed, Emma put her plate to one side then picked up a square of paper towel and pressed it carefully to her lips.

'It's OK, Em. My father told me he'd invited you. He made a point of it, in fact. Just like the old man to dig the knife in and twist it. Well? Did you have a good time?'

His calm expression obviously belied the maelstrom of resentment that was tearing him up inside and Emma's heart thudded painfully against her ribs at the knowledge.

'Yes.' She nodded, her expression guarded. 'It was good. What did you mean when you said it was just like your father to dig the knife in?'

Lawrence scowled. 'He was playing games, Emma. Didn't you realise? I don't want to hurt your feelings but he only made a play for you because he knew I liked you.'

All of a sudden Emma's chest felt very tight and she found it hard to breathe. 'What are you saying? That your father deliberately set out to seduce me to get his own back on you?'

'Think about it, angel. Why else would he show such an interest in you? I mean, you're a good-looking girl and all that but my father is used to dating beautiful women. And they're usually models or CEOs or socialites—women in the strata of the mega-rich. I've never known him to date a waitress before.'

If he had physically struck her, Emma couldn't have felt the pain of the blow more.

'I never realised until now how much of a bastard you can be, Lawrence.' Tears in her eyes, she jumped to her feet and crossed her arms in front of her chest to stop her hands from trembling.

As her hurtful gaze skimmed his youthful good looks and tousled blond hair, she didn't have to wonder where Lawrence had inherited his appeal. He had the stamp of his illustrious father all over him and had broken a fair few hearts already to her knowledge—but it was only now that she was beginning to recognise the ruthlessness that must run in the Redfield bones. They didn't seem to care who they hurt or used as long as they got their own way.

'I didn't mean that to come out the way it sounded.' As he rose to his feet, Lawrence's gaze was immediately regretful. 'You know it's just him I'm mad at.'

'And that's supposed to excuse your vindictiveness towards me?' Her dark eyes furious, Emma could hardly speak across the pounding of her heart. 'What am I? Some kind of prize to you both? Since when did I stop being a person with a life of my own?'

'Em, please.'

'Don't you dare "Em" me! I think you're despicable. And so is your father! If I never set eyes on either of you again I will consider myself blessed!'

Lawrence took a swig of his drink from the soda can then wiped his mouth with the back of his hand.

'Why did you sleep with him, Emma? You knew how much I liked you.' His blue eyes openly resentful, he didn't even seem to register Emma's insult. When she didn't immediately reply to his question, he shrugged and looked as if he wanted to hit somebody. Emma automatically took a couple of steps back.

'I don't need anyone's permission to do anything! And if you liked me so much, why did you constantly parade a stream of girls in and out of this flat as if you were running some kind of harem?'

'You know why. I needed physical gratification and you wouldn't give it to me.'

'You're exactly like a spoilt child. You think you should be able to have whatever you want and to hell with the consequences!'

'You could be describing Piers himself.' Letting loose an unpleasant little smile, Lawrence took another swig of his drink, crumpled the can in his hand and jettisoned it into a nearby packing case. 'For God's sake, Emma! My father has been able to have his pick of women since I was young. What do you think drove my mother so crazy? She was intensely jealous and only had affairs to pay him back. He may have spent most of his time working but it's obvious he didn't go without female company.'

'So I'm just another notch on his belt, is that what you're saying? Albeit one that's beneath him on the social scale. Well, you needn't worry, Lawrence, because it meant nothing…really. You can tell him that when you next see him. Not that he'll care.'

Suddenly weary with the weight of emotion that was dragging her down, Emma just wanted to find some peace. She would think about all the implications of what Lawrence had said tomorrow. Right now all her defences were down because she lacked the mental energy that was required to keep them in place and all she wanted to do was curl up on her bed and lose herself in sleep. Smoothing down her jeans, she headed for the door. Lawrence caught up with her just before she got there, his hands locking on to her wrists to impel her towards him.

'You deserve better than him,' he told her huskily, his gaze moving restlessly across her startled face.

'What do you mean?' Alarmed, she tried to pull her wrists free, but Lawrence wasn't in a hurry to let her go.

'Come to Cornwall with me, Em. What's holding you here? Don't mind me saying, but now that your grandmother's gone you can please yourself, can't you? You'll easily get a job and even if you don't I can support you until you do. You can be my muse... You know you've always inspired me!'

Emma stopped struggling to free herself and stared at him instead. 'You can't be serious. What about Vicky?'

'She's gone...finished. Told me she had an aversion to anywhere that wasn't London and had no intention of moving somewhere as unhip as Cornwall. Can you believe it?'

'Lawrence, do you really think I'd go anywhere with you after the things you've said to me this evening? Think about it—'

Her words were cut off by Lawrence's lips on hers, his tongue catching her unawares, diving inside the soft, moist cavern of her mouth with all the clumsiness and ardour of a boy on his first date. Emma was initially too stunned to push him away, so neither she nor Lawrence heard the soft knock behind them or saw the man who stepped inside the door that had been left slightly ajar until it was too late.

'Conveniently, I found the front door left unlocked. I hope I didn't walk in on anything important?'

'Piers!'

'I'm gratified you remember my name. You certainly don't let the grass grow under your feet, do you, Emma?'

As she jerked out of Lawrence's embrace as though she'd been slapped, Emma's face turned pale. Piers looked as immaculate as ever, in a black overcoat on top of yet another exquisitely tailored suit, and his gaze was direct and unflinching and about as unforgiving as stone. Nervously drawing the sides of her red wool cardigan together across her blouse, Emma shivered, unable to find words to defend herself.

'I—I thought you were going away for three months?'

Observing her pallor and the shock in her big brown eyes with a strange mixture of regret and white-hot fury, Piers swallowed hard. That Emma should betray him cut like a knife—but that she should betray him with his own son was like being flayed alive. Right now he didn't know who he was more furious with—Emma or the feckless Lawrence.

'So you thought the way was free and clear for you and Lawrence to get together?'

Appalled, Emma felt her mouth drop open. 'I thought no such thing! Lawrence…say something, for God's sake!'

Before his son could say anything Piers interjected, 'As it happens, my plans changed. Well, Lawrence…aren't you going to say anything? It's partly because of you I changed them in the first place. Would you care to tell me exactly what's going on?'

Her brow puckering in confusion, Emma turned to glance at Lawrence, who grabbed up another can of soda and took a swig from it, as if nothing in the world could possibly be amiss. 'All's fair in love and war, Dad. You weren't here in Emma's hour of need—now, why does that not surprise me? And *I* was…simple as that. Em's going to come down to Cornwall with me and stay with me a while, aren't you, Em?'

'I'm doing no such thing!' Not knowing whether to laugh or cry, Emma was furious that she was somehow caught in the middle of some psychological game Lawrence was playing with his father. And what had Piers meant when he'd said he'd changed his plans because of Lawrence?

'Is something going on between the two of you?' Turning his head towards Emma, Piers knew he couldn't deny the evidence of his own eyes. Not when he'd seen Lawrence kissing her senseless. But he wanted to hear confirmation from her own lips just the same... Those sweetly luscious lips that he had craved the taste of from practically the moment he'd seen her and was *still* craving. Yes, he'd partly axed his travel plans because of Lawrence—somewhere along the line the two of them had to start building bridges and if it wasn't now, when Lawrence was planning a new start away from all he knew in London, then when would they work things out? But mostly Piers had come back because of Emma. The thought of her was like a mantra in his mind that refused to go away, and he had to address the fact or die wondering.

'We're just friends. At least, I *thought* we were. If Lawrence has other ideas I assure you they are nothing to do with me.'

At her irritated answer, Piers let out his breath another notch. Shrugging carelessly, Lawrence simply grinned at them both. 'Can't blame a bloke for trying, can you?'

'So you kissed Emma to take a swipe at me, is that it?'

'One-upmanship, Pops...plain and simple. It felt good to have something that you wanted. It was worth it just to see the look on your face!' His sarcastic tone undercut with anger, no longer smiling, Lawrence threw his now empty soda can into a nearby empty cardboard box, where it bounced once then fell to the side. Scraping his fingers through his tousled blond hair, he glanced briefly down at the floor before continuing as if trying to contain his temper.

'The only reason you've come back into my life is because of Emma. You couldn't give a damn whether I sink or swim, could you? You never could. Then I find out you took her to Paris…a woman *I* was interested in! You think giving me money fixes everything but I've got news for you—it doesn't! All it does is make me despise you even more!'

'Since when did you want anything more from me than money?'

His crisp, cultured tones commanding attention even though he hadn't remotely raised his voice, Piers considered his son with an ice-cool glance that could cause frost-bite and which Emma knew instinctively must crush any opposition in his business dealings. But zinging through her brain first and foremost was Lawrence's admission that he had been trying to get one over on his father by kissing her. He must have set her up… He must have been expecting Piers—otherwise, why the conveniently left-open front door? Not to mention the door to the flat… At the very idea that Lawrence could have stooped even lower than he had already without so much as a single thought for her welfare, Emma felt her stomach recoil in dismay.

'You knew Piers was coming, didn't you, Lawrence? You weren't concerned about me not eating at all… You just wanted to use me as some kind of ammunition against your father in this stupid game you're both playing! How could you?'

'I don't want to hurt you, Em. I meant it when I asked you to come to Cornwall with me and I *am* concerned that you haven't been eating properly. I know how much your grandmother meant to you. Whatever you think of me I'm still your friend.'

'No, you're not. You're just a user, Lawrence. I guess it must run in the family.'

Trying hard to give Piers a wide berth as she rounded

him to reach the door, Emma didn't miss the scalding glance he gave her as she accidentally nudged his arm, and her heart jumped wildly in her chest.

'Don't go far, will you?' he warned. 'You and I have some unfinished business.'

Unable to bring herself to speak for the tumult of emotions crowding her chest, Emma hurried out the door and banged it shut behind her.

Back inside her own flat she made a half-hearted attempt at some ironing, her whole body tensing at every sound she heard from upstairs, flinching when the two men's voices were threateningly raised, listening intently when things went ominously quiet. Sighing, Emma switched on the radio for distraction, then grew tearful when she inadvertently tuned in to a programme her grandmother had loved. When over an hour had passed and all seemed peaceful upstairs, she finally put away the iron and went into the kitchen to make a hot drink. Her gaze alighting mournfully on the damp-riddled walls, she felt as if they were closing in on her and knew a sudden deep desire to escape. Where to didn't matter because right now her poky little flat was a too painful reminder that she was more or less going nowhere with her life. Before her grandmother died she'd kidded herself she stayed there because it was all she could afford, but now that Helen Robards was no longer around Emma really had no excuse not to make a change. God help her, at this moment even going to Cornwall with Lawrence was more appealing than staying put.

But of course she would never really consider such a thing. Notwithstanding the look of disbelief and rage that Piers had worn on his face at the sight of her in his son's arms, after his recent behaviour Emma wouldn't trust Lawrence as far as she could throw him. But in the light of what she had learned from him, that surely now went for his father too.

The brief knock on her living-room door almost made her wish there were somewhere to hide. She could pretend she wasn't in but there was no way Piers would buy that. Threading her fingers anxiously through her hair, Emma went to answer the door, her mouth going dry at the thought of being alone with Piers for the first time since they'd returned from Paris.

He stepped inside without saying a word, his clear blue eyes taking a silent inventory of her haphazard living-room, making Emma wish that she'd cleared up a little before he appeared. But why worry when she wouldn't be inviting him to stay?

'You look terrible.'

It wasn't what she'd expected to hear and it hurt. 'Thanks.'

'I didn't mean that the way it sounded.' Rubbing his hand around the back of his collar, Piers took a stride towards her, seemed to think better of it then shrugged off his overcoat instead.

Emma swallowed hard. 'What do you think you're doing?'

'I'm going to help you pack.'

'Pack?'

'You don't think I'm letting you stay here all by yourself in that condition?'

'That's the second time you've insulted me in the space of two minutes! For your information I'm fine. What do I need to pack for? I'm not going anywhere.'

'Yes, you are.' Piers's jaw was resolute as his exasperated gaze swept over Emma's troubled features. Throwing his coat onto her couch, he loosened his tie and pushed a hand through his dark blond hair. 'You're coming home with me, and don't waste your breath giving me an argument because my mind's made up and you won't change it.'

CHAPTER TEN

WHEN she'd recovered from the shock of his ultimatum, Emma turned and marched into the kitchen. Opening the fridge, she took out a carton of milk, placed it on the counter, then delved into the cupboard beneath the sink to find a saucepan. Piers appeared in the doorway just as she reached into another cupboard for the tin of chocolate powder she kept there.

'What are you doing?'

'Making a bedtime drink—what does it look like?' she snapped.

'Didn't you hear what I just said?'

'Listen, you may be lord of all you survey at work but that doesn't apply to me! I'm not going anywhere with you and I'm quite capable of taking care of myself. You must think I'm some kind of simpleton, that's all I can say! You have the barefaced audacity to waltz in here as if you own the place and order me about when you coldly and calculatingly used me to get back at your own son! Why I even let you through the front door I don't know, but I'd be grateful if you just turned around and left. I'm sick of your games, Piers, and your son's. Just go away and leave me alone.'

His face went white. 'So Lawrence did his worst, did he?'

Emma swallowed hard. 'He told me that you took me to Paris to score a point. Do you know how that makes me feel, Piers? Have you any idea?'

He had the grace to flinch. Lawrence had inadvertently

found out about the trip to Paris from Fiona, Piers's PA. He'd rung to speak to his father and Fiona had told him he'd gone away for the weekend. Apparently Lawrence had made some quip about 'business or pleasure?' and Fiona had let slip that he'd taken a girl called Emma Robards. He'd had the full story from Lawrence just now upstairs, and had been appalled when he'd learned that his son had put his own damning slant on it. Piers might have started out wanting to compete for Emma's attention, but he had not succumbed to trumpeting his victory under his son's nose. Yet perhaps he deserved that Emma believed he did.

'I didn't tell him I took you to Paris. He found out from my secretary. You must know he was only looking for an excuse to damn me in your eyes.'

About to tell him that Lawrence had succeeded in doing just that, Emma caught the flash of remorse in Piers's troubled blue eyes and wearily decided against it.

'You know, the more you two fight the less likely it is you're ever going to reach a resolution. Don't you think life's too short for all this upset?' As she pushed her hair back from her forehead, the skin around Emma's mouth looked pale and strained and her eyes profoundly tired. An acute pang of regret hit Piers somewhere deep in his solar plexus.

'I'm sorry about your grandmother. It must have been a terrible blow.' His softly articulated words made her stop what she was doing and her hand clutched the tin of chocolate powder as if it were the last defence against him and her grief.

'It was.'

Piers shifted from one foot to the other, his gaze genuinely sympathetic yet his expression not inviting confidences. Instinctively Emma guessed he was not entirely sure how to handle her grief.

'And I'm also sorry for that cheap little stunt that Lawrence pulled just now. I wish I could have spared you that.'

'Is he still mad at you?' Emma wanted to know.

'We've got some way to go before we resolve things but we've had a long talk and hopefully we've made a start.'

'He had no right to use me like that just to score points against you.'

'Believe me, I don't condone what he did.' If it had been any other man besides his own son, Piers would have been ready to be violent, such was the jealous rage that had gripped him. 'I don't suppose you plan on forgiving him any time soon?'

Emma honestly didn't know. Right now she was feeling hurt and more than a little let down by her supposed friend. 'We'll have to see how things go. From where I stand at this moment, he's got a long way to go to redeem himself in my eyes.'

'He suspects that already. He thinks a lot of you, Emma. You've been a good friend to him.'

'As crazy as it may sound I don't dislike him...even now.'

'He's a good-looking young man. I could hardly be surprised if you did find him attractive.'

Emma lifted her head in surprise. His arms folded across his chest, Piers leant against the doorjamb, his perceptive blue eyes plainly keeping watch for any noticeable signs of too-eager compliance.

'Well, I don't. I'm afraid he's a little too immature for me.'

'That aside, I don't think many girls would find it a hardship to be kissed by Lawrence.'

Didn't he have any idea that Lawrence the boy couldn't hold a candle to Piers the man? Emma was truly bewildered that Piers could even suggest that she might prefer his son's immature kisses to his own.

'"Handsome is as handsome does," as my gran used to say. I told you before, Lawrence and I are just friends—though God knows you'd never believe it with the way he's carried on lately.'

'Don't make the mistake of thinking that he doesn't care about your good opinion of him. From what I've seen I can tell he does. He saw an opportunity to get back at me in some way and he took it. I really don't think he thought of it as using you. Believe me, he knows now it was the wrong thing to do.'

Had Piers been jealous when he'd found her in his son's arms? Emma dismissed the thought as quickly as it had arisen. She wouldn't make the mistake of thinking she meant something to either him *or* Lawrence again. They both seemed to regard her as some kind of possession, that was all—and a disposable one at that.

'So you've agreed on some kind of a truce?' she asked.

Piers nodded. 'We've both agreed to let down some barriers. We've got to if things are going to improve.'

Sucking in a surprised breath, Emma let it out again slowly. 'You'd be willing to do that?'

'Perhaps I'm not as intransigent as you think I am.' The little half-smile that played around his lips made Emma's insides tighten and the front of her thighs grow warm.

'That's good...really. At least it will be a start. I never got the chance to get to know my father. He left when I was nine.' Brushing back her hair again with her hand, Emma turned back to the counter. She marvelled that her voice could sound so steady when all she could really think about was Piers holding her, letting her lean into some of that seductive strength of his for a while. She imagined him stroking her hair and telling her that everything would be all right, because she really believed that if this man would deem a thing so, then it would be. For her he undoubtedly had that much charisma; that much power…

'And you've no idea where he is?' Frowning, Piers wondered if this was what Emma had been referring to the first time he'd made her acquaintance—when she'd commented, 'some of us are struggling with deeper issues.'

'Not specifically. I mean, I don't have an address or anything but as far as I know he's in Australia. He wrote to my grandmother when he first went over there but he moved around a lot and they soon lost touch. He's made no attempt to contact me in all these years, and now I can't even let him know that his own mother is dead.'

Studying her slim, straight body, the dark chestnut hair that gleamed even under that unforgiving fluorescent light, and the weight of sadness that was clearly weighing her down, Piers no longer questioned whether he had done the right thing in cancelling his trip abroad. When he'd rung Lawrence to try and make some kind of restitution for his previous lack of contact, during the course of their conversation his son had casually blurted out, 'By the way, Emma's grandmother has died. I think it's hit her pretty hard.' Remembering the touching sight of her arrestingly beautiful dark eyes illuminated by tears in the Parisian café that rainy afternoon, Piers had experienced such a powerful need to see her that almost as soon as his call to Lawrence was at an end, he'd rung his deputy and instructed him to make the scheduled trip abroad in his place. It was the first work-related trip that Piers had cancelled for many a long year, and if his young deputy had been surprised by his decision, he'd done a remarkable job of not revealing it.

Clearly Emma needed time to come to terms with her

grandmother's death, but Piers had no intention of letting her do it here in this depressing, dingy little flat with its peeling wallpaper and damp patches on the walls. He was even more adamant about that when he considered that she might actually be pregnant with his child. The thought commanded such unexpected feelings of protectiveness that even though he refused to stop and ask himself why, Piers was determined to do the right thing by Emma... whether she welcomed it or not.

'Well, make your drink if you insist but then you're going to go into your bedroom and pack. I'm not leaving you here on your own to brood when you can have the run of my house with all your meals cooked and Miles to take you wherever you want to go. Oh, and before we leave, I want the name and telephone number of your land-lord.'

Inwardly bristling at being dictated to again, Emma swung around, her desire for the hot chocolate she'd been going to make gone completely. 'Now, wait a minute! I told you I'm not going anywhere with you, and why on earth do you need the name and telephone number of my landlord?'

'Because I'd like a little chat with him about letting his property go to rack and ruin. It's a health hazard living in a place this damp, Emma. Don't you know that?'

Glancing up at the offending areas on the walls, Emma shrugged to hide her embarrassment. It shamed her to see her home through his critical eyes. She knew he was right about the landlord reneging on his responsibilities, and yes, damp *was* a health hazard. She only prayed he wouldn't have cause to use her bathroom because it was worse in there. But underlying her embarrassment was resentment that he naturally assumed he knew what was best for her.

'Of course I know that! I've rung my landlord more

times than I care to mention to tell him about the damp and ask that he do something about it but he always fobs me off with some excuse. Look, Piers, we said goodbye at the airport and I assumed that was the last we would see of each other, so why do you imagine you have a perfect right to just walk in here and start telling me what to do? Never mind. Whether you stay or go I've got things to do.'

Intending to brush past him, Emma was shocked when Piers started to walk towards her, his forbidding expression as intractable as rock.

'If you're expecting my child then I have every right to be concerned about the conditions you're living in—not to mention responsibility for your welfare.'

Stunned by his words, Emma felt her mouth drop open. Since her grandmother died she'd barely given the possibility that she might be pregnant a second thought. She hadn't dared. Already hurting because Piers had been so distant with her when they'd said their goodbyes at the airport—as if their lovemaking had never even happened—she hadn't wanted to make herself even more miserable by fearing the worst. But now when she thought about it...would it really be the end of the world if she was to find out she was pregnant with Piers's child? What if it was a new beginning instead? At least she would have someone of her own to take care of. For a girl with no family at all, it was the first ray of hope she'd had since being told by the surgeon that he'd been unable to save her grandmother. Practicalities about how she would support herself flew out of the window as the thought flourished in the frozen soil of her bereaved heart and took root.

Closing her mouth, Emma swallowed hard. 'We don't know that. And I'm *not* your responsibility, no matter what. Now, I'm asking you again to just go, Piers. I'm very tired and there's so much to do. I've got piles of my grandmother's correspondence to deal with as well as my own, and if I don't begin somewhere I—'

'Don't you ever listen?' Suddenly his face was very close to hers and Emma backed up against the counter, her heart starting to thud alarmingly. But even though he intimidated her, a renegade pleasure was racing through her bloodstream, making her tremble with longing. His nearness had the power to totally banish every other thought in her head and make her long to be in his arms instead. In a million years she'd never dreamt of begging a man to make love to her but right now, with Piers, Emma was so close. It would be so good to experience some pleasure again, she thought longingly, even if it was only temporary—because the last few days had been pure hell. Her face suffusing with heat, she dipped her head to shield her hungry gaze before it betrayed her. 'I'm not going with you, Piers. It would—it would be wrong.'

'Wrong for who?' Suddenly Piers had to touch her. He drew his fingers gently down the softly velvet surface of her cheek, tipping up her chin so that she was forced to look at him. The pupils of her distinct honey-brown eyes had grown arrestingly dark and he saw her delicious, plump lower lip quiver slightly. Heat exploded inside him like a small incendiary.

'You need taking care of.'

'No, I don't.'

'Good God, woman! Are you going to argue with me the whole night long?'

There were other things Emma would much prefer to do with him all night long but she had neither the confidence nor the strength to state it—not with his nearness making it hard for her to take a breath, let alone talk.

'No.' Her voice had diminished to a husky whisper and

Piers's hypnotic mouth curved into a deep smile, highlighting dimples that she hadn't even realised were there. Piers Redfield, powerful, admired head of one of the country's foremost management-consultant firms, had dimples. *Dimples,* if you please! And they softened every firm slash of cheekbone and jaw and transformed merely handsome into heartbreakingly unforgettable...

'Good.' The smile vanished and he stepped away, his blue eyes alight with satisfaction and some other undisclosed feeling she wasn't privy to. 'Now go and pack while I clean up the kitchen and get this place straight before you leave it.'

Wide-eyed, Emma pushed away from the counter and wondered what Piers's esteemed colleagues would think of their boss now as he rolled up the sleeves of his immaculate white shirt and prepared to get stuck in to Emma's washing-up. She couldn't quite believe the evidence of her own eyes herself.

'You don't have to...' But she cut short her argument when, with one razor-sharp flash of those devastating blue eyes, Piers effectively squashed any further dissent and made her suddenly welcome the relative sanctuary of her bedroom.

Curled up in one of Piers's too comfortable fireside chairs, a good blaze burning in the large bricked fireplace warming her legs, Emma briefly shut her eyes and wished she could simply allow herself to doze a little. But in the luxurious large kitchen, with its solid light oak floor and sea of marble worktops that would put The Avenue's workspace to shame, he was currently making her the mug of hot chocolate she hadn't got around to making at home. As she opened her eyes once more, Emma's appreciative gaze absorbed the stately beauty of her surroundings and she tried to imagine living in such a house all by herself as Piers did—well, when he wasn't travelling around the world, that was. With its obviously cherished antique furniture, high ceilings and ornamental balcony looking out on to a large private garden—a garden that Piers had promised her would be at her disposal any time she wished to enjoy it—she felt a little like Alice in Wonderland. But wouldn't a person get lonely living in such a grand house by themselves? No matter how beautiful it was, it couldn't make up for the warmth of human companionship, could it? Frowning at the nagging pain in her temple, Emma pondered the fact that she had so easily allowed Piers to persuade her to come here, knowing that if she hadn't been feeling so tired and weak she would have put up a better fight to stay where she was. But whatever his motives for inviting her to stay in his house, admittedly she was glad not to be alone tonight for a change.

'I hope I've made it how you like it.' Suddenly he was there in front of her, carefully transporting her mug of hot chocolate on a tray that he placed on a small cherry-wood table by her side. When Emma started to sit up and uncurl her legs from beneath her, Piers waved her back down again. 'Stay right where you are. You look far too comfortable to move.'

His smile was unguardedly friendly and startled Emma out of her sleepiness. At home he seemed far more relaxed and at ease in his surroundings yet she couldn't help wondering again if he didn't get lonely living by himself. Being estranged from his only son couldn't help either, even if he didn't admit it. Everyone needed someone.

'You're right. I *am* too comfortable to move. Although I shouldn't really be here at all.'

'That's a matter of opinion.' Walking across to the fire then staring thoughtfully down into the crackling flames,

Piers looked preoccupied for a moment before turning his head to regard her. He experienced a heady rush of pleasure at her beauty when he did and his gaze lingered in admiration at the way her silky dark locks fell in soft waves onto her shoulders, and the way the firelight danced in her liquid brown eyes. Then it struck him how right she looked ensconced in that big fireside chair, and in a completely unguarded moment he thought about seeing her there every evening when he came home…

'I'll stay until tomorrow then I really must go. I've got post I haven't even opened yet and I must write thank-you notes to all the people who came to the funeral…' Breaking off from her anxious list of things to do, Emma rubbed at her temples with her fingers, her growing headache making her wince. There hadn't been that many people at the funeral but still her grandmother would have wanted her to do the right thing and thank them.

'I put all your post and correspondence in a carrier bag and brought it with us. You can look at it tomorrow if you insist but you're not going back to that damp apartment until I get the landlord to do something about it.'

'That's hardly your responsibility!'

'Forgive me if I beg to differ.' Walking across the room to the drinks cabinet, Piers splashed some brandy into a glass then returned to stand in front of the fireplace.

'No wonder Lawrence finds you impossible to deal with!'

Refusing to be baited, Piers couldn't help but smile. 'Don't start this argument with me, Emma, because you won't win. Now, why don't you just sit back and enjoy your drink and when you're ready I'll show you upstairs to your room?'

Willing herself to move, Emma reluctantly straightened

in her chair and reached across to the side-table for her hot chocolate.

'I don't know why I'm doing this.'

'Yes, you do.' For an electrically charged moment Piers caught and held her defeated gaze. 'You're here because for once in your life you need someone else to take the reins for a while—worry over you for a change.'

Was he worried about her? Emma found the prospect far too difficult to believe. He was only behaving the way he was towards her because he had some misguided sense of responsibility in case she was pregnant with his child. As soon as they both found out she was not, he would leave her alone to get on with her life just as she had been doing before he showed up...

'I don't need anyone to worry over me.' Taking an experimental sip of the mouth-watering hot chocolate, Emma found she welcomed the sweet warmth that slid over her tongue, down her throat and into her stomach. She shouldn't have been surprised to learn that the man they dubbed a corporate wizard was not completely undomesticated, but to tell the truth she was.

Although amused by her stubbornness, Piers simply didn't buy Emma's emphatic statement that she didn't need anyone to worry over her. The girl had just lost the person who was closest to her. If that wasn't bad enough, she lived in a dingy little flat with damp on the walls and was facing the prospect of possibly becoming a single mother—all because Piers hadn't been able to curtail his lust long enough to think about protection. He might not be able to fix everything in her life but when it came to living in more salubrious surroundings in better accommodation—and in the future possibly a better job with more prospects—well, he could do that much for Emma, couldn't he? Swirling the brandy in his glass, he studied her as she sipped her drink, knowing that if circumstances had been different and he'd invited her to his house for the night in the ordinary way he would have without a doubt wanted to make love. In fact his whole body was thrumming now with the need to do so—like a battery left on charge. But studying her now, her eyelids drooping as she forced herself to stay awake, Piers knew this was one occasion when he wouldn't put his own needs first.

'Drink up and I'll take you upstairs and show you to your room.'

'Will you be going in to your office tomorrow?' Emma asked him warily.

'No.' His reply was emphatic, and Piers smiled as if to underline it. 'From tomorrow I'm planning on taking a few days off.'

Placing her half-consumed drink back on the table, Emma tucked her hair behind one ear and sighed. 'Then in that case, if I can borrow a clock I'll set the alarm and be out from under your feet just as soon as I can.'

'No, Emma. You're not running away that easily. I've already told you you're staying here as my guest until your feckless landlord undertakes some proper repairs to his property.'

'But that could be months!' Her eyes widened in alarm.

'Then so be it.'

Helping herself to another sugar in her tea, Emma read the formally worded script of the solicitor's letter again to make sure she had got the content right in her mind. Emma was requested to attend tomorrow afternoon at the offices of Arbuthnot, Johnson and Harris in the West End to hear the reading of her grandmother's will. Helen Robards had survived on a widow's pension all these years, and her granddaughter knew only too well that there had been very little money left over for anything else save day-to-day living expenses—let alone savings. But her grandmother had always asserted that, when the time came, she would leave the house to Emma. She'd barely given the matter a thought in the days since the funeral. While she was still reeling from her loss, material gain was the last thing on her mind. Now, taking a sip of the hot, sweet tea that Mrs Mayes, Piers's housekeeper, had made her, Emma put down the letter for a moment to glance admiringly around the abundantly stocked library. As well as being a dream come true for anyone who was passionate about books, it was a stunningly beautiful room with two sets of large Georgian windows looking out in genteel fashion on to a verdant landscaped garden that seemed to stretch for miles. Her gaze captured just then by a charming little robin that had flown onto a nearby window ledge, Emma didn't immediately hear the door open and Piers walk into the room.

'How's the headache?'

Her heart jolted at the sound of his deeply resonant voice and as her gaze made contact with his, Emma was struck again at how shockingly blue his eyes were. He was casually dressed in a cream cable-knit sweater and blue jeans, and the less formal clothing seemed to accentuate his attractiveness even more.

'It's fine… I mean, it's gone. Mrs Mayes gave me two paracetamol and that seemed to do the trick.' Every time he glanced her way Emma felt as if she became a tongue-tied schoolgirl. The sooner she got back to her flat and resumed work at the bistro the better, as far as she was concerned. Only every time she tried to raise the subject of her returning home, Piers was adamant she wasn't going until her landlord had undertaken the repairs Piers deemed necessary.

'Good. You're looking a little brighter today at least.'

Gratified at the rosy hue in her cheeks, even if the central heating was mostly to blame, Piers sensed something inside him relax. He'd lain awake most of last night preoccupied with thoughts of the lovely young woman sleeping just down the corridor from him, planning what he would do should she find herself pregnant. He'd buy her a house not far from his own, he'd decided. Then he'd hire a nanny to help with the baby so that Emma wouldn't get too worn out in the early days and still get some much-needed sleep. Remembering how Naomi had fared just after she'd had Lawrence—how tired she'd looked, how much she'd complained to Piers that motherhood was just too much, that she'd felt trapped at not being able to come and go as she pleased—he experienced a deep pang of regret that he hadn't been around more to help her. But in those days his determination to be successful, both professionally and financially, had driven him to be away from home much more than he might have strictly needed to be and eventually he'd paid the price for neglecting his young family. Piers wouldn't let Emma suffer in the same way. OK, so she'd be a single mother, but he'd see to it that she and the baby didn't go without a thing.

'I've got an appointment tomorrow afternoon.' Suddenly uneasy with his attention, Emma latched on to the solicitor's letter and snatched it up off the Davenport. 'The reading of my grandmother's will.'

'Miles will take you. Just tell me the time and I'll arrange it.'

He was being so polite, so solicitous, and Emma wanted to scream at his formal tone. If he was going to be so distant in every other way, why did he have to stand so close to her? So close that she breathed in the sexy, lingering scent of his aftershave with every breath and—most unsettling of all—the languid, virile heat from his body.

Did Piers imagine for even one second that Emma was immune to all that? Did he truly believe that she had forgotten the unremitting lust that had overtaken them at the café and driven them back to the hotel so urgently, not even allowing them to make it as far as the bedroom before desire had its way?

'Thank you.' Miserable because he seemed to have wiped any recollection of that desire clean from his memory bank, Emma folded her letter and slotted it back into its cream envelope without another word.

'Mrs Mayes is preparing lunch for one o'clock... That all right with you?'

Sinking against the chair back, Emma nodded wearily. 'That's fine. Thank you.'

'You don't have to thank me for everything.' Piers's penetrating blue eyes appeared even more intense than usual. A muscle throbbed in the side of his smooth temple, making Emma aware that underneath that outwardly formal manner there was a lot more going on than she realised. Was he angry with her? She wondered why.

'How do you want me to behave?' she asked in frustration. 'I'm here in your house, you won't let me lift a finger to do anything and I don't think you realise just how much I have to do at home—not to mention at my grandmother's house! She spent over forty years in that house; can you imagine the clearing out I've got to do?' It all welled up inside her then and tears spilled from her eyes before she had a chance to check them. Even the thought of going back to the little house she knew and loved so well to do that final task for her grandmother made her feel as if someone had ripped out her heart and carelessly put it back again broken and bruised. Before she knew it, she was sobbing hard.

Piers acted immediately. Drawing her up from her seat

where she sat head bent in despair, he gathered her close into his chest, kissed the top of her head and rubbed her back. All the while he crooned gently that he would take care of everything, that she mustn't worry because everything was going to be all right.

And then…everything changed. His lips moved helplessly from the top of her head to the side of her tear-stained cheek beneath her softly scented dark hair, and Emma glanced up, surprised, and made a little sound, a sound raw with hope and longing and need…

CHAPTER ELEVEN

IT WAS her eyes that undid him. It was a rare woman whose beauty intensified in distress but Emma was that woman. Her soft, honeyed gaze tore at Piers's heart through the curtain of her tears and made him ache for something meaningful and good in his life again. Something like this woman, who could reach inside him like no other… Unable to help himself, he let his mouth descend on hers and drank deeply from the well of her essence, his passion and desire inflaming as she yielded to him with all the generosity of spirit he knew she had in her. And in that moment Piers wanted her as he'd never wanted another. When her small, slender hand started to caress the small of his back, circling his skin through his sweater as she pressed her pelvis flush against his, he tore his mouth from hers and groaned.

'Emma…' As he cupped her face between his hands, his glance could have started an inferno. 'If you keep on touching me like that we're going to wind up in bed for the rest of the afternoon and that's not why I brought you here.'

'I know.' Because emotion was locking her throat, Emma's voice was a bare whisper—a throaty sound that belonged to someone else. 'But what if that's where I want to be with you?'

Visibly affected, his mouth softening, Piers slowly let his hands slide down her face to her shoulders. 'Are you sure, Emma? You've been through a bereavement; it's understandable if you feel confused.'

'I'm not confused, Piers...at least, not about this.'

'Whatever you want, Emma, I'll give you. You only have to ask.'

His words giving her courage, Emma swallowed down the last of her tears and gently let her fingers glide against his lips. 'I want you to touch me. I want you to make me forget this awful thing has happened for a little while. Will you do that for me?'

Sliding in between perfectly laundered crisp white sheets, Emma shivered as she waited for Piers to join her. When he reached out to draw her into his arms, the heat of his skin seemed to scorch her everywhere it came into contact with her own. Her hands gliding over him, she loved the feel of hard, resolute muscle beneath skin that was surprisingly soft—his forearms and chest dusted with fine blond hair that was anything but rough. With exquisite tenderness, Piers handled her as if she was something infinitely precious that might break if he made so much as one wrong move, and Emma was deluged by her need for him. But underneath that undoubted tenderness was a river of passionate molten steel that was growing stronger at every touch, every stroke. While she sensed it and rejoiced in the knowledge, gasps of pure hungry pleasure broke loose unrestrained from Emma's lips—soft, breathless, eager sounds that seemed to inflame Piers even more.

The first time with her he'd been too hasty, too avaricious to take what he so urgently desired with any real finesse. Passion had made him its slave and he'd been mindless and reckless and possibly put her in a predicament that neither of them wanted. This time it would be different. Now, as Piers allowed his gaze to make a slow, sensual inventory of her loveliness, he silently acknowledged that her nakedness was a wonder to him—every delicious curve and line of her beautiful body a fascination. With waves of glossy dark hair rippling across the pure white pillow, her eyes growing darker and more inviting with every stroke and touch of his hand, Piers felt a raw shiver of pure delight shudder through him before he lowered his head to kiss her. As soon as he made contact an explosion of sensation washed over him, more deeply affecting than any kiss he'd ever experienced before. In her lips was enough magic to keep a man well contented not just in this life but in many other lifetimes too. She teased him with her tongue, sliding it damply across his mouth before melting him inside, then ran her hands up his arms and locked on to his biceps—a little press here, a sensuous slide there, the tips of her lovely breasts tantalising him with every brush against his chest. Everything about this woman aroused his desire. Her scent had surely been created just to drive a man wild, let alone what she did to him when she touched him.

'Piers…' The soft little whisper in the shape of his name fluttered against his earlobe like a butterfly's breath, teasing him and sending goose-pimples scudding in all directions, hardening him even more.

'What is it, you little seductress?'

'Am I?' Momentarily Emma stilled, awed at the concept of her own power, her long-lashed eyes round with wonder as she stared up at him in the dimmed light created by the drawn curtains.

'Of course you are.' His acknowledgement was low and husky as he reached down between them, parted her thighs and slid into her with one hotly possessive, powerful stroke. Emma arched in surprise, her breath leaving her body in a long, shuddering gasp.

'You could look at any man and make him want you. But right now, Emma…you belong to *me*.' As he moved

inside her, momentarily silencing her with his fiercely possessive affirmation, Emma slid her arms across his powerful shoulders, secretly delighting in the strongly contract-
ing muscles rippling beneath her hands. Then she found
herself praying that the afternoon would stretch long into
the night and help her forget her sorrow for just a little
while. He would never love her in the way she yearned
for him to love her, but if all they ever had was this breathtaking, earth-shattering joining together—then she would
have to be content. What else could she do? She would
simply have to bear it, even though she knew now with
certainty that what she felt for this man was not some
passing passion that would fade in a few days, months,
years even. Her heart was his, even if he never found out
the truth. After today, she would guard her feelings with
more care, not let him see that if she had to walk away
from him one more time it was probably going to be the
hardest thing she'd ever done. He had ruined her for any
other man that came along in the future but even that
Emma would surmount because she was strong—stronger
than she had thought she was. Circumstances had made
her that way and nothing was going to bring her down or
make her feel *less than* ever again.

Tomorrow she would buy one of those pregnancy tests
from the chemist and put herself out of her misery. She
was only two days late for her period but once she knew
the result for sure she would take action and begin to see
just what she was capable of—because wasn't that what
her beloved grandmother would have wanted for her?

The solicitor's office hadn't been too difficult to find,
tucked down a short side-street amid bars and restaurants
not far from bustling Leicester Square. Miles got her there
bang on time, telling her he would go and get a cup of

coffee somewhere before returning to the car to wait for her. Inside the rather gloomy offices of Arbuthnot, Johnson and Harris, it was hot and stuffy and surprisingly old-fashioned. With its antiquated furniture in the waiting-room and a rather foreboding receptionist with a cut-glass accent that reminded Emma of an old-style school head-mistress, after the cosmopolitan noise and colour of the streets outside it was like stepping into another world. When Emma was briskly shown into the necessary office, she could just about see the short bespectacled little man with his military-style black moustache that inhabited it behind the mounds of papers and files that threatened to topple over on his desk.

'Ah, Miss Robards. So pleased to meet you.' Standing up, he briefly shook her hand then waved her into the rather tattered red leather chair that was made available for clients. Seated once again, Mortimer Harris, as he'd intro-duced himself to Emma, made a brief but interested as-sessment of her neatly attired figure as she opened her coat, his gaze finally settling on her outwardly calm, pale com-plexion with apparent satisfaction. 'Well, let us not waste time, eh? I am sure you are as anxious to hear the reading of your grandmother's will as I am to avail you of its contents…'

After that Emma fell into a kind of numbed silence, and when she left the office just twenty minutes later she was still reeling with disbelief at what she had heard.

The heels of her smart but despised high heels clicked against the polished black and white marble floor of the large, imposing entrance hall. Emma thanked Mrs Mayes for letting her in then immediately forgot to ask the affable housekeeper if Mr Redfield was at home. Sighing as the woman's own retreating heels echoed down the hall into the distance, Emma stood for a moment to gather her thoughts, automatically slipping off her shoes and flexing her throbbing toes with relief at the blessedly cold marble beneath her feet. A little shiver ran down her spine. What would Piers's reaction be when she told him that besides being left her grandmother's house she'd been left twenty thousand pounds from her absent father? *Twenty thousand pounds...* She still couldn't take it in. But right now the thought brought Emma little joy. She'd discovered from the solicitor that Helen Robards had written to Emma's father when she was seriously ill and appealed to him to help his daughter. It had come as a shock to learn that her grandmother had known her son's whereabouts all this time but had kept it from Emma because he expressly hadn't wanted to be contacted. Now she also learned that her father *still* didn't want any contact with his child. The money was a one-off payment he'd clearly made out of deference to his mother—not because he wished for a chance to renew his relationship with Emma. Conscience money...that was what it was. For a moment rage and distress made her dizzy. The bastard hadn't even sent flowers to his own mother's funeral.

Clamping her hand to her head, Emma told herself she was better off without him. Conscience money or no, at least now she would be able to support herself and the baby, should she find herself pregnant... The thought made her tummy swim anxiously for a moment. In her bag was a pregnancy test she had purchased at a local chemist, and as soon as she got the opportunity she would do the test and see once and for all what she had to deal with. Either way, she'd made her mind up about one thing. As soon as she could talk to Piers she would tell him that she was going back to her flat—damp walls or no damp walls. She couldn't bear being in limbo any longer. Besides, the sooner they made a clean break the better. Piers could go back to the high-octane corporate world he knew and loved, and Emma could get on with her life—maybe even think seriously about undertaking some further education. With her grandmother's legacy, that was no longer out of the question.

'You're back.'

'Yes.' Startled by his sudden appearance, Emma felt an answering shiver roll down her spine. Yesterday they'd been outrageously self-indulgent, spending nearly the whole of the afternoon in bed, and last night Piers had still not tired of making love to her. Today her tingling body— more alive than it had felt in years—definitely registered the after-effects of his passionate attention. So much so that Emma could hardly bring herself to look him in the eye without her cheeks shading a revealing rose-pink— even if he was smiling at her as if he was remembering her willing and naked in his bed and maybe wanting to take up where they had left off...

'Did everything go all right?' he asked conversationally. No other man could make an ordinary black sweater— even if it was cashmere—and jeans look so good, Emma decided.

'Yes, fine. We have to talk. Can you spare a few minutes?'

Piers wondered that she had to ask. Right now he'd postpone pretty much everything to spend time with her and much to his surprise had actually found himself relishing the time away from work. Nothing and nobody had ever effected such a change before.

'Of course. Come into the library. Mrs Mayes has lit the fire and if we're lucky she'll bring us a cup of tea shortly.'

Helping her off with her coat, Piers smiled to himself

as he glanced down at her stockinged feet minus her shoes. One day soon, he vowed, he would buy her a pair of high heels that wouldn't hurt her feet. Something classy and expensive that would make her endlessly long legs look even more sensational.

Making herself comfortable in one of the fireside chairs, Emma immediately stretched out her hands towards the glowing coals in the grate. Her complexion was flushed from the cold wind outside and her eyes were as bright as topaz. Folding her coat over the back of his chair, Piers sucked in his breath with deeply male satisfaction at her beauty—opting to stand for the moment as he waited for her to speak. He could only hope that all had gone well at the solicitor's because God knew the woman didn't need any more bad news.

'It seems that I'm a woman of means. My gran always said she was leaving her house to me but I also received some money from my father.'

'Your father?' Piers's eyes narrowed in surprise.

Emma dipped her head. 'When my grandmother knew she was going to have to face a major operation she apparently wrote to him and asked him to help me. I never even knew she knew where he was. He sent money to ease his conscience but he still doesn't want anything to do with me.'

Absorbing the news with strangely mixed emotions when he knew he should be fiercely glad for her good fortune at least, Piers was taken aback by the sudden little niggle of disquiet that arose in him. That it might have something to do with the fact that if she now had means she might decide she didn't need his help, he refused to consider. But there was also the fact that she was clearly perturbed by this new turn of events concerning her father.

'He's the one who's lost out, Emma. As for the rest…well, you deserve it.'

Compared to the losses she had suffered, her grandmother's death and her father's desertion, Emma wondered how she was supposed to derive any satisfaction at all from her unexpected legacy. Feeling suddenly terribly cold, she rubbed her hands briskly together in front of the fire to warm them. 'So you think I should just accept the fact he doesn't want to have anything to do with me and keep the money?' she asked quietly.

'Of course.' The fact that she would even contemplate not keeping it was so typically Emma that Piers could hardly be surprised.

'Will you give up your job at the bistro?' he asked.

'Why? What's wrong with my job?'

'We're not back to that old chestnut again, are we?' Exasperated, Piers briefly turned his back on her to stem his temper. 'Why should I care what you do for a living, Emma? I'm not your keeper!'

'No,' Emma agreed softly, rubbing her trembling hands down her soft wool skirt. 'You're not. I can do just as I please, can't I? In fact, that's the main reason I wanted to talk to you. I've decided to go back home to my flat. There really isn't any good reason for me to stay here any longer, is there? I mean, I'd rather get on and do the things I need to do than stay here getting under your feet. I'll go and pack my things and—'

'No.'

'What do you mean, no?'

Startled, Emma glanced up in surprise as Piers planted his feet squarely in front of her, glaring down at her with the full force of those crystalline blue eyes. 'I told you I'd prefer it if you stayed under my roof until your landlord gets those repairs done. I spoke to him this morning and he's sending a contract hire team in to do the work starting from tomorrow. So you see, you can't go home yet. The flat's going to be in chaos for at least the next three weeks or so.'

'Three weeks?' Emma blinked. 'Why is it going to take three weeks? They've only got to do something about the damp.'

'Not so. They're completely redecorating as well as putting in a new bathroom and shower.' He'd seen the horrendous damp on Emma's bathroom walls the day he'd sent her into her bedroom to pack and the bathroom suite had clearly come out of the ark. Piers hadn't wasted a second in reading her landlord the Riot Act about the conditions his tenant was living in, and using his not inconsiderable name as leverage to get every one of his demands met. Piers was only thankful that Lawrence was getting out of the place to move to Cornwall. The whole house should be condemned, in his view. If he had his way, he'd move Emma out of there for good as well.

'He must be cursing my name.' Wincing at the idea of her notoriously mean landlord receiving that particular phone call from Piers, Emma glanced down at her linked hands and shook her head. 'You shouldn't have gone to so much trouble on my behalf. And what about my personal things? I should go and sort them out if they're going to be moving things around to decorate.'

'I've already left strict instructions that if anything goes missing or is broken I will hold your landlord one hundred per cent accountable.'

Emma didn't doubt he would by the stern glitter in his eyes. 'I'll still need some more clothes. I didn't bring nearly enough with me.'

'I'll buy you some new ones. It's not a problem.'

She didn't suppose anything was if you happened to be

Piers Redfield. 'Well, if the flat is uninhabitable for the next three weeks, I'll simply go to my grandmother's house and stay there, then.'

But even as the words left her mouth, Emma didn't think she could face going to the house just yet. Not when her feelings were still so raw.

'I want you to stay here. It makes sense, doesn't it? It's warm and comfortable. Mrs Mayes and Miles are both on hand to help, and I'm here to help too—that goes without saying.'

Their gazes met and locked, with Emma being the first to look away. It wasn't his help she was craving. Reaching for the moon was what she was doing and it was a waste of time. The longer she stayed in Piers's house, the harder it would be for her to leave. Their relationship didn't have a future—how could it, when he was who he was and she was way down the scale of women deemed suitable for a man in his position? He'd made it perfectly clear from the beginning that theirs was just a brief affair, so there was no way she was going to hang around feeling hopeful…not unless she didn't mind having her heart ground down into the dust.

'I'm sorry but I can't stay.' Shakily, she rose to her feet, sweeping back a silky dark tendril of hair that refused to behave itself. 'I really can't.'

Short of locking her in the house and being charged with kidnapping, Piers realised there was nothing else he could do to force Emma to stay. But the idea of her leaving to go back to an empty house with too many memories to haunt her was almost too much for him to contemplate. Last night, holding her in his arms as she dozed gently beside him, he had actually dreaded letting her go. That had never happened with any other woman since his early days with Naomi, but the idea that he might at long last

be needing someone in his life permanently after all these
years was not one he willingly entertained. His was a responsible position and his work was everything to him
and—to be brutally honest—the idea of marrying again
filled him with apprehension. Look what a disaster he'd
made of his marriage to Naomi! She'd been too young to
be tied down with a baby and so was Emma. He'd be crazy
to even consider repeating the same mistake—especially
considering the effect it had had on his son. Piers took
pride in giving one hundred and ten per cent to his work.
Could he jeopardise another relationship with the unre-
lenting demands of his job just because he imagined he
was mellowing in his old age? He didn't think so.

'Then, if you insist on going, I'm going to book you
into a nearby hotel. At least you'll have some of the com-
forts of home and I can still keep an eye on you. Let me
make a phone call and see what I can fix up.'

'You don't need to do that. I'm perfectly capable of—'

'Emma.'

That coldly commanding gaze of his was surely designed to instil immediate compliance, but it incensed
Emma. 'What?' She rolled her eyes heavenwards.

'You have only two options. Either you stay here under
my roof or you let me book you into a hotel. What's it to
be? Tomorrow I'm helping Lawrence move down to the
West Country and I need to know what you've decided
before I leave.'

'You're helping Lawrence?' Once again Emma felt as
if the wind had been taken out of her sails.

'Don't look so stunned. He can't do it all on his own.
We've hired a removal company to do the bulk of the
lifting and carrying but he's still going to need help sorting
it all out when he gets there, and besides...I want to see

the place he's renting. He might need a few things. I'll probably stay overnight and drive back the following day.'

It was because he was helping Lawrence that Emma decided not to give him an argument after all. The idea that father and son were hopefully on the road to reconciling warmed her heart, making her feel glad that at least one relationship was being sorted out. 'I don't want you paying for me to stay in a hotel, so I guess I'll stay here. But if at any point my presence becomes an inconvenience, I insist you tell me straight away. Is it a deal?'

Transfixed by that sexy little beauty spot at the top of her left cheekbone, Piers couldn't help the pure smile of gratification that curved his lips. 'Deal. But this is a big house, Emma. I don't see how it's possible for you to inconvenience me in any way. By the way, I've got a couple of friends coming over for dinner tonight—think you can face some company?'

Emma would really rather not, but because he was still smiling and she didn't want to break the mood, she found herself agreeing. 'Why not?' she said.

Blinking at the pink box of the test stick, Emma raised her gaze to stare dazedly into the bathroom mirror. Overwhelmed with relief one moment, her face crumpling in dismay in the next, she angrily scrubbed the tears from her eyes and threw the offending test-stick into the little sea-grass wastebasket. So she wasn't expecting Piers's baby after all. The knowledge made her feel oddly hollow, as if a vital part of her body was suddenly missing. Now there was no reason—no reason at all—for him to maintain contact after Emma vacated his house in three weeks' time. She would have to walk away and never see him again. With Lawrence taking up residence in Cornwall, they would have no reason to even set eyes on each other. The tension in her ribcage making it difficult to breathe, Emma shuddered out a deeply affected breath then went out into the adjoining bedroom to reluctantly dress for dinner.

Eve and Doug Webster were Piers's oldest friends. Doug and he had worked together briefly before he gave up the corporate world to start a business of his own—a charming little hotel in the Cotswolds that was going from strength to strength. Occasionally, when he could spare the time, Piers stayed there and one would be hard put to find a more charming hostess than the lovely red-haired Eve. It was a rare occasion indeed when Piers was able to invite his friends to his home as he was always away so much, so he had been delighted when they'd said they could come. Now, as they laughed and talked over dinner, Piers was acutely aware of the fact that Emma had hardly said a thing. Not only that, but she had hardly touched the delicious food Mrs Mayes had prepared either. She was sitting opposite him next to an effusive Doug, a brief smile touching her perfect lips at some hilarious story Doug was relating, but behind her smile Piers sensed an even deeper sadness than usual and couldn't dispel the feeling of anxiety that crept into his bones. Had she changed her mind about staying with him? Was she going to tell him after his guests had left that she was leaving after all? Studying her face in the candlelight, Piers couldn't prevent the powerful stab of possessiveness that knifed through him. She couldn't leave him. Not yet…

'You haven't heard a single word I've said, have you, Piers?' Taking a generous slug of red wine, Doug narrowed his merry brown eyes suspiciously at his friend. 'So…have you got something you'd like to share with Eve and me?'

His gaze suddenly sombre, Piers didn't flinch from the

other man's searching glance. 'What are you talking about?'

'Well, all you've done throughout dinner is gaze at the lovely Emma—not that I blame you for a moment, mind. She *is* rather gorgeous.'

'Steady, lover-boy, or you'll be going home on your own tonight.' Her stunning green eyes flashing, Eve Webster glanced from her husband to Emma and grinned good-naturedly.

'So, *have* you got something you'd like to tell us about you and the lovely young lady by my side, or haven't you?' Doug persisted. Beside him, Emma let her gaze gravitate to Piers, meeting his burning blue response with understandable trepidation. It was an intensely awkward moment but she couldn't help but be interested in how he was going to explain her presence here to his friends.

'Emma is a friend…that's all.'

Her insides turned to ice at his almost dismissive words. Of course, she hadn't expected him to elaborate on their relationship, but to be so heartlessly dismissive, as if she was hardly worthy of mention… Forcing herself to smile, Emma fought back her hurt and shrugged. 'That's right. We're just…friends.'

CHAPTER TWELVE

SHE escaped shortly afterwards on the pretext of needing the bathroom. The few stolen minutes in her room on her own, gathering her thoughts, helped Emma make up her mind what she was going to do. Pulling the ivory-backed hairbrush through her hair—part of the beautiful antique set that Piers had provided for her use—Emma sat in front of the dressing table, shocked at how pale she appeared. There were deepening shadows beneath her eyes and her skin looked thin and stretched, just as she felt inside.

What she needed was a holiday, and, since she now had the money to enable her to have one, that was exactly what she was going to have. Tomorrow she'd go into town and book a flight to the sunniest tropical place on the globe she could find, where she could relax and plan what she was going to do next with her life. It was the perfect time to go. Her flat was being redecorated and wouldn't be ready for occupation for another three weeks and she couldn't face going back to her grandmother's house just yet. But most of all her desire to escape boiled down to one thing—Piers didn't really want her in his house and he most certainly didn't need her. How could Emma believe he did when he'd clearly been highly embarrassed at the idea his friends might find out his real relationship with her? 'Emma is just a friend,' he'd said—if you read between the lines, nobody of any account.

Hugging her arms around the thin white silk blouse that she'd matched with black velvet trousers, she fought back the pain cramping her throat, opened the door and went soft-footed down the winding staircase to rejoin the others in the drawing-room. Just as she reached the door she heard Eve exclaim, 'She's a waitress? Oh, Piers!'

Her stomach turned over with a sickening lurch. She could just imagine what was going through the Websters' minds right now. Were they laughing at her behind her back? Perhaps amused that a girl who was a mere waitress thought she was good enough to hobnob with the likes of such exalted company? Was Piers laughing too? The force of her anger making her tremble, Emma withdrew her shaking hand from the brass doorknob to try and compose herself. When Mrs Mayes suddenly appeared beside her carrying four filled champagne flutes on a silver tray, the kindly housekeeper's warm hazel eyes swept over Emma with concern. 'Are you all right, Miss Robards? Aren't you feeling well, dear?'

'I'm fine, thank you. I just needed a little air. Let me take those for you.'

'Oh, no, dear, I—'

'Please.' Emma flashed her warmest smile. 'I insist. I was just going back inside anyway.'

Reluctantly Mrs Mayes released the tray into Emma's capable hands. 'Thank you, dear, that's very kind. Enjoy the rest of your evening, won't you?'

A moment later, Emma swept into the room with the tray of drinks. Eve and Doug were seated either side of the beautiful, imposing fireplace as she entered, while Piers stood by one of the tall Georgian windows, looking somehow restless, as if he had too much energy to merely sit still. Perhaps he was having regrets about offering her the hospitality of his home? Maybe he'd come around to thinking it might be better if he just let her go after all— especially if her presence was going to make him feel awkward in front of his friends. She was sure it wouldn't be

long before he found someone to replace her anyway…
Her heart welling with hurt, Emma tried to calm her rising
temper, as the glasses on the tray had started to rattle
alarmingly.

'Emma?' He seemed surprised to see her with the tray,
his handsome face serious as she answered him with a
brittle little smile.

'Yes, Piers?'

'What are you doing carrying that? I asked Mrs Mayes
to bring in the champagne.'

'What's the matter? Embarrassed at the reminder of
what I do for a living?' Her dark-eyed gaze defiantly
swinging from Piers to the couple seated either side of the
fireplace, Emma put the tray down carefully on the coffee-
table and straightened angrily. 'I'm not going to apologise
for what I do to anyone! I'm a damn good waitress, if I
say so myself, and I've got nothing to be ashamed of!
Funny how in company I'm suddenly not good enough,
isn't it? You didn't seem to think so when I was in your
bed!'

'What nonsense is this?'

She sensed his rage even though there was a good six
feet plus of dark blue Aubusson carpet separating them,
wondering how he managed to convey such steely com-
posure when he was obviously smouldering with anger
inside. But, of course, he was ever the smooth, unruffled
professional, she realised—the only time she'd ever really
seen him let his guard down remotely was in bed.

'It's not nonsense! I heard you laughing at me.'

'Emma, darling, I didn't mean to—' Eve Webster got
to her feet, her hand pressed in alarm to the V of her pretty
emerald-green blouse.

Before she could continue, Piers interjected, 'Will you
excuse us for a moment? Emma and I need to have a little

talk.' He had moved across the room with a stealth that took Emma by surprise and now, with his hand firmly anchored beneath her elbow and deliberately ignoring her mutinous glare, he guided her purposefully from the room.

'What the hell was all that about? Do you think my friends give a damn what you do for a living?'

'Let go of my arm!' Emma fumed, wrenching her elbow free. 'I don't care to be manhandled!'

'Don't be ridiculous.'

'Oh, I'm ridiculous now, am I? As well as an embarrassment?'

Looking as if he was mentally counting to ten, Piers let loose a heavy sigh and pushed his fingers through his hair.

'You've embarrassed nobody but yourself with that little scene just now.'

A red mist in front of her eyes, Emma couldn't stop the emotion that was pouring through her like white water. 'Of course. How could I be so stupid? A man who doesn't feel anything can't possibly be embarrassed, can he? You probably surround yourself with friends who are just the same. All wearing your social masks like the pros you are! Too afraid to come out and rub shoulders with real people now and again in case the experience taints you in some way!'

Pausing to draw breath, Emma saw with alarm the tiny throb of muscle in Piers's smooth forehead. Wondering this time if she'd gone too far, she concluded that if she was going to make a dramatic exit from his life then she might as well go for broke because she was convinced now that she definitely didn't have a future that included Piers Redfield. His comment at dinner that they were 'just friends' had confirmed it.

'You think I don't feel things?' he challenged, his eyes

emanating little sparks of blue ice. 'Your opinion just demonstrates you don't know the first damn thing about me.'

'And why is that?' Her brows shooting up to her hairline, Emma glared back at him. 'You made sure right from the off that you were a closed book as far as I was concerned. You gave me access to your body and your house and your car but not your mind or your heart! No wonder Lawrence could never get through to you—no wonder he had to resort to cheating and lying and playing stupid games to get your attention! You're the original iceman, Piers. You don't understand such a concept as "need." You don't need anybody or anything and you damn well like it that way!'

'You don't know what the hell you're talking about.'

'No? You sit up there in your ivory tower, acting as if you run the world—making sure your staff keep out the riff-raff. Not only that, you think you can buy whoever you want with your wealth. You're as bad as my father, assuaging his conscience with blood money! Did I forget myself for a minute and imagine I was your equal just because you deigned to notice me?' As she dropped a mocking curtsy, Emma's dark eyes flashed her disdain. 'Please, sir, forgive me, sir, I'm your humble servant, sir!'

His temper near to exploding, Piers locked his hands around her upper arms in her thin silk blouse and yanked her hard against his chest. Before she had time to protest he extinguished any further dissent with a hotly passionate, furious kiss, his heart racing as he felt her initial resistance melt and her body sink bonelessly against his. When he withdrew his mouth, her breath was escaping in soft little gasps against his skin and all the blood in his body had only one destination in mind.

'I've got many faults, Emma, but I hope thinking I'm better than anyone else isn't one of them. And I've certainly never tried to buy someone's affection with money. I know who I am, what I stand for and where I've come from. For your information my father was a labourer and my mother a school cook, and my friends Eve and Doug? They're both in the catering business. In fact Eve started out her career as a waitress herself. I've rubbed shoulders with ''real'' people all my life and having money and a high-powered career hasn't changed that.'

Wishing that the ground would open up and swallow her, Emma shakily extricated herself from Piers's embrace and took a less than steady step away from him. Her lips throbbed and ached from the brutal passion of his kiss and her treacherous body couldn't seem to help craving his touch the way a starving man craved food. But her overriding emotion was deep and profound embarrassment that she'd humiliated herself so badly.

'But I thought—'

'You thought you weren't good enough to meet my friends because they were somehow above you. Isn't it about time you lost that chip on your shoulder?'

'I—'

'Don't pretend you don't know what I'm talking about. Your self-inflicted feelings of inferiority are stopping you from getting on with your life, Emma. Have I ever honestly made you feel that I looked down on you in any way because of what you do?' His jaw clenched, Piers was still clearly furious and, try as she might as she gazed anxiously into his eyes, Emma couldn't seem to get her heart to regain its natural rhythm.

'No, but—'

'Then don't look for reasons to confirm your poor opinion of yourself where there aren't any.'

Was he right? Emma wondered. Had she been putting up barriers without even realising it? Had she made her fears self-fulfilling? She'd been hiding behind that chip on her shoulder for so long, it had become a habit she should have dumped long ago.

His countenance unsmiling, Piers shook his head slowly from side to side. 'Take five minutes to compose yourself,' he advised, his expression grim. 'Then, when you've calmed down, come back in and join the company.'

Biting back a hurt retort and feeling like a naughty schoolgirl who had just been severely rebuked by the headmaster, Emma returned upstairs to her room—her throat unbearably tight, angry tears making her eyes sting.

Emma hadn't returned to join Piers and his friends that evening and she most certainly hadn't calmed down. Now, in the early hours of the morning, spooning coffee granules into a mug as she waited for the kettle to boil in the huge, luxurious kitchen, she told herself he must have been relieved when she didn't reappear. Certainly at no point had he come to her room to try and persuade her to join them. Emma stared off into space, her stomach churning with the possibility that he might have finally written her off for good. How could she possibly redeem herself in his eyes after she had accused him of so many dreadful things? Her stomach groaned at the thought. Now he probably couldn't wait to be rid of her. It didn't help her frame of mind that her body was aching with all the heartfelt longing of a creature yearning for its mate whenever she thought of Piers. Telling herself it was probably for the best that they hadn't ended up spending the night together under the circumstances, she vowed to let him know her plans today and make a clean break. She threaded her fingers through her newly washed hair, a forlorn sigh escaping her, the very thought making her heart feel as if it was weighed down with lead.

The door opened as if on cue and suddenly the object of her thoughts was there in the flesh—looking for all the world as if he'd enjoyed the sleep of the innocent, handsome and devastating in dark blue jeans and a charcoal-grey crew-neck sweater. For a moment speech deserted Emma. Then, desperately trying to gather her wits, she managed a nervous little smile.

'You're up early.' Hugging her chest, she wished with all her heart that she were properly dressed, instead of standing there in just her nightwear. She felt vulnerable enough without her skimpy clothing giving her a disadvantage.

'I'm going to Cornwall today with Lawrence. Remember?'

At the sight of her slim, shapely figure attired only in her very fetching eau-de-Nil nightdress and wrap, her long dark hair curling damply over her shoulders, Piers felt all the heat in his body shift commandingly to his loins. So much for the supposed effectiveness of ice-cold showers. He hadn't wanted to stay away from her last night, but after her outburst earlier in the evening he'd convinced himself she needed some breathing space. Now he wished he'd convinced himself otherwise. In any case he'd hardly slept. It just didn't feel right not to have her there in his arms, sharing his bed. All night long he had been restless for her touch. Then finally, in the early hours, when it was still as black as coal outside, Piers had pushed aside his covers, headed straight for the bathroom and braved a full twenty minutes beneath a freezing cold shower in a bid to try and curb his lustful craving for Emma. Now, looking at her, he knew it hadn't worked. If he hadn't agreed to help Lawrence to move today, he would be persuading her to come straight back to bed with him and wouldn't let her go until he'd convinced her that her beauty and desirability had no match.

'Of course. He must be so excited. It's his dream to go to Cornwall and make his living as an artist.'

'Whether he'll make a living out of it remains to be seen, but I guess you can't fault him for trying.'

His unexpected grin tied Emma's stomach into severe knots. She blushed helplessly, disconcerting heat seeming to flood her limbs. 'I'm glad that you're both getting along better. Parents and children should always try to reconcile their differences, in my view. Once your parents are gone, you don't get another chance.'

Once again Piers sensed the sadness in her and found himself wishing with all his heart that he could do something to ease it. 'Maybe one day your father will decide to get in touch, Emma. You should never give up hope.'

'I doubt it. He's made his feelings on the matter perfectly clear, wouldn't you say?' There was a fleeting flash of pain in her beautiful dark eyes, then she shrugged it off as if it had never been and smiled. 'Anyway, I wanted to tell you that I won't be here tomorrow when you get back, and it's not because I'm not grateful that you've offered me a place to stay while my flat's being decorated. It's just that I've decided I need a holiday. And maybe… maybe it's time we properly parted company? You have the demands of your work and Lawrence, and I—I really need to think about what I'm going to do with my life now that I've suddenly found myself with some new options.'

'And what about the very real possibility that you might be pregnant with my child?' The blatant possessiveness in his tone stung Emma like the lash of a whip and for a moment it completely threw her. Trying to force her words past the arid desert in her throat, she lifted her shoulders and dropped them again as if defeated. 'I'm not pregnant. I did a test... I was going to tell you last night but you had company and then we rowed and...'

The disappointment and dismay that welled up inside him momentarily hijacked Piers's breath. Up until that moment he hadn't realised just how much he'd been secretly hoping that Emma was carrying his child. Granted, it made no sense when he'd been vowing for so long now that he never wanted to be a father again—not when he'd made such a hash of it the first time around. But somehow with Emma the idea had crept in that this might just be a new chance for him. A chance not only to be the father he wished he'd been all those years ago when Lawrence had needed him the most, but also to be a better husband. The kind of husband a woman would be proud of...

'Aren't you going to say anything?' Her soft voice cut through the sudden mist in his brain, forcing Piers to focus. *Husband?* Now, that was a big shift of focus. One he clearly needed time to assimilate.

'I expect you're relieved.' Those wide shoulders of his lifted in an almost careless shrug. It wasn't quite what Emma had expected him to say but clearly he must be feeling immense relief himself. Why wouldn't he be? Now there was no longer any need for him to feel obligated to her in any way. Just in case there was, she decided to leave him in no doubt. 'Yes, I am, as a matter of fact.' She straightened, turning her back on him on the pretext of needing coffee when all she really needed was him. 'I'm going to take this holiday and when I get back I thought about enrolling in college to do something.'

'College?'

He was finding it hard to string a sentence together. Her assertion that she was relieved had cut him to the quick. Hadn't she been furious with him in the restaurant in Paris when he'd suggested she couldn't possibly be happy about the prospect of being pregnant? Now she was talking about going back to college—worse still, about 'properly parting company.' Piers didn't like this new turn of events one little bit.

'I need to get some qualifications if I want a change of career.'

'And that's what you want now, is it?' His voice was unknowingly brittle. 'A career?'

Emma couldn't understand why Piers seemed so hostile about her plans. Pouring hot water into the blue ceramic mug on the counter, she wished her hand wouldn't tremble so, but the thought that these might be the last few moments she had with the man she loved was frankly almost too much to bear. In just a short space of time Piers had somehow become essential to her whole existence and even the prospect of a holiday in the sun and enrolling in college on her return could do nothing to lift her spirits. Would he find it easy to forget he'd even known her? Emma shivered miserably in her inadequate wrap and cupped her hands gratefully around the steaming mug of coffee.

'I've hidden behind my job at the bistro for long enough,' she confessed. As she turned to face him her teeth worked anxiously on her vulnerable lower lip. 'I convinced myself I wasn't really good enough to do anything else. And then when my grandmother became ill and I had to help care for her, I told myself there was no point in even thinking about a new career. You were right. I did have a chip on my shoulder. Now I know I'm not pregnant I can take the opportunity to make things better for myself—at least put wheels in motion to get a new job.'

On the other side of the large, luxurious kitchen, Piers's expression was scathing. 'So...motherhood never really did hold that much appeal?' Even as he posed the question, his heart felt as if it were being crushed in the hands of an invisible giant. It was so hard to block out the mental picture he'd been forming of Emma pregnant with his child, radiant and beautiful; both of them planning a future together… But how could he suggest such a thing when she was clearly so relieved not to find herself in that state?

It was at that very moment that Piers finally had to admit the truth to himself. He loved her. He'd been fascinated by her from the very beginning when she'd shown up in his office to plead Lawrence's case, and that fascination had slowly but surely transformed into love even though there had been so many times he'd fought to deny it to himself. Emma was so wrong about him. He *did* need her. He needed her as much as he needed to breathe. But now, as she revealed that she wasn't expecting his child, that she was however planning a holiday and a new life—a life that obviously didn't include him—Piers knew it was time to let some barriers down. Even risk rejection, because the idea of living without this woman was killing him.

'I didn't say motherhood didn't hold any appeal. One day perhaps, when I meet the right person, I—'

'The right person? Damn it, Emma! What the hell do you think you're playing at?' In just a few long strides he was in front of her, taking the mug of coffee out of her hands and plonking it down on the counter, uncaring that the hot liquid splashed him, his intimidating blue eyes scorching her with their hungry intensity, his hands gripping her waist and impelling her body roughly against his own. 'You can't just walk out on me as if what we had meant nothing! You might have been bearing my child… Damn it, don't you know I wished you were?'

Before Emma could orient herself with what was happening, her mouth was crushed beneath the smouldering heat of his lips and she opened it helplessly for him, uttering a husky little groan of acquiescence between the clash of tongues and teeth, her body trembling so hard that she couldn't hear herself think. All she knew for sure was that her love for this man was the axis her whole world spun on.

'Do you mean it?' Calling a reluctant halt to their kiss a few seconds later, her hands resting on his lean, hard hips beneath his woollen sweater, Emma stole an anxious glance into that mesmerising sea of blue, her heartbeat speeding up all over again when his lips curved into a seductively melting smile. 'You really wish I was having your baby?'

'I love you.' Watching her lovely brown eyes widen in shocked surprise, Piers lifted her damp, silky hair aside to plant a hot little kiss on the side of her neck, the scent of her warm, velvet-soft skin rising up to captivate him and saturate his senses in heady desire. Spellbound, he lifted his head to simply gaze at the face he loved and, when he saw her heart reflected right there in her steady, loving gaze, was frankly astounded that Emma's feelings seemed to run as deeply as his did for her. 'I want lots of babies with you, Emma...but only if you want them too. Naomi was too young when she fell pregnant with Lawrence. Motherhood and being a wife made her feel trapped. I would hate to think that I would inflict that same feeling on you.'

Taking all of half a second to discount the very idea, Emma sighed and slid her arms lovingly around his neck. 'Oh, Piers! I want children too, and there's honestly no fear of me feeling trapped. Maybe for your wife it wasn't the right thing to be a mother so young, but I'm a different person, Piers. I know my own mind. I was distraught when

I found out I wasn't pregnant. Don't you know how much I love you?'

'Well, I'm hoping you're going to spend a lot of time convincing me, Miss Robards. Especially after accusing me of being…what was it you said? "The original iceman." I have feelings for you deep enough to drown in, my angel. If I seemed aloof it was because I was scared of committing to another woman again after Naomi. I spent a long time feeling terribly responsible for the way her life worked out.'

'You're a good man, Piers. I'm sure you didn't deliberately make life difficult for her…and I'm sure that wherever she is now…she would want you to be happy.'

His heart squeezing with regret at what had happened to Naomi and at the same time brimming with love for Emma, Piers knew he had to finally make peace with himself. Just as he had advised Emma to lose that chip on her shoulder, he now had to take his own counsel, forgive the sins of his past and embrace the future with hope.

'There's only one thing.' Looking for all the world like a reluctant child about to confess to some minor misdemeanour, Emma curled her fingers into the soft wool of Piers's sweater. 'I know in this day and age it might be considered a little old-fashioned, but I really don't agree with having children out of wedlock. Is that a problem?'

'Are you proposing to me now? Brazen hussy!' Chuckling, Piers kissed the top of her head then bestowed the same treatment on her lips, his pulse quickening at the sight of her pink-cheeked response. 'Of course I want us to marry…and if you don't mind, I'd rather not take too long about it either.'

'But Piers…what about Lawrence?'

'What about Lawrence?' His heart stalling at the idea that Emma might be having second thoughts because of her past relationship with his son, Piers waited with trepidation for her to explain.

'How will he take the news, do you think? I don't want to be the cause of any more animosity between you.'

'Lawrence will take it on the chin,' he told her with relief. 'Now that we've agreed to work together to put things right I'm hopeful that things are improving between us. But what about you, Emma—will you mind being stepmother to your friend?'

'It will be strange at first, but I expect we'll both get used to it in the long run.' Snuggling into him, her head on his chest, Emma felt the strong, steady beat of his heart against her ear and offered up a silent little prayer of gratitude. *We've both been given a second chance to get it right,* she thought in wonder. They'd both been tormented by life-changing events in their pasts. Now together they would have a chance to heal.

'Let's go back to bed,' Piers whispered before lifting her head to gaze into her eyes.

'We can't. You're helping Lawrence move today, remember?' Regretfully Emma sighed, the idea just too tempting to be borne.

'How much do you want to bet me he isn't even up yet? And besides...' Grinning wickedly, Piers slid a hand behind her back and started to lead her to the door '....we may not have much time before I have to leave, but who says it won't be damn satisfactory just the same?'

Michelle Reid

Jane Porter

Susan Stephens

One Christmas Night

On sale 3rd December 2004

Available at most branches of WHSmith, Tesco, ASDA, Martins, Borders, Eason, Sainsbury's and all good paperback bookshops.

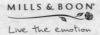

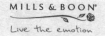

MILLS & BOON®

Live the emotion

1104/01b

Modern
romance™

THE MEDITERRANEAN PRINCE'S PASSION
by Sharon Kendrick

He was like the hero of a film. He had rescued her, made love to her... But now Ella had discovered who he was: Nicolo, daredevil Prince of the Mediterranean island of Mardivino! Nico was used to getting what he wanted – and he wanted Ella...

THE SPANIARD'S INCONVENIENT WIFE *by Kate Walker*

Ramon Dario desperately wants the Medrano company – but there is a condition: he must marry the notorious Estrella Medrano! Ramon will not be forced into marriage, but when he sees the gorgeous Estrella, he starts to change his mind...

THE ITALIAN COUNT'S COMMAND *by Sara Wood*

Miranda still loves her estranged husband, Count Dante Severini, and misses him and their son. Dante wants to be rid of Miranda, but their son misses her. Dante issues Miranda with a command: she must live with him and act as the perfect wife...

HER HUSBAND'S CHRISTMAS BARGAIN *by Margaret Mayo*

When Italian businessman Luigi Costanzo discovers that his beautiful estranged wife is the mother of his child, he is furious! How dare Megan keep his daughter from him? Megan is unimpressed when Luigi turns up, just before Christmas – but he is hard to resist...

Don't miss out...

On sale 3rd December 2004

Available at most branches of WHSmith, Tesco, ASDA, Martins, Borders, Eason, Sainsbury's and all good paperback bookshops.

MILLS & BOON

**Volume 6
on sale from
3rd December
2004**

Lynne
Graham

International Playboys

*The Winter
Bride*

WE VALUE YOUR OPINION!

YOUR CHANCE TO WIN A ONE YEAR SUPPLY OF YOUR FAVOURITE BOOKS.

If you are a regular UK reader of Mills & Boon® Modern Romance™ and have always wanted to share your thoughts on the books you read—here's your chance:

Join the Reader Panel today!

This is your opportunity to let us know exactly what you think of the books you love.

And there's another great reason to join:

Each month, all members of the Reader Panel have a chance of winning four of their favourite Mills & Boon romance books EVERY month for a whole year!

If you would like to be considered for the Reader Panel, please complete and return the following application. Unfortunately, as we have limited spaces, we cannot guarantee that everyone will be selected.

Name: _____

Address: _____

_____ Post Code: _____

Home Telephone: _____ Email Address: _____

Where do you normally get your Mills & Boon Modern Romance books (please tick one of the following)?

Shops ❑   Library/Borrowed ❑

Reader Service™ ❑ If so, please give us your subscription no. _____

Please indicate which age group you are in:

16 – 24 ❑   25 – 34 ❑

35 – 49 ❑   50 – 64 ❑   65 + ❑

If you would like to apply by telephone, please call our friendly Customer Relations line on **020 8288 2886**, or get in touch by email to readerpanel@hmb.co.uk

Don't delay, apply to join the Reader Panel today and help ensure the range and quality of the books you enjoy.

Send your application to:

The Reader Service, Reader Panel Questionnaire, FREEPOST NAT1098, Richmond, TW9 1BR

If you do not wish to receive any additional marketing material from us, please contact the Data Manager at the address above.

FREE

4 BOOKS AND A SURPRISE GIFT!

We would like to take this opportunity to thank you for reading this Mills & Boon® book by offering you the chance to take FOUR more specially selected titles from the Modern Romance™ series absolutely FREE! We're also making this offer to introduce you to the benefits of the Reader Service™—

- ★ **FREE home delivery**
- ★ **FREE gifts and competitions**
- ★ **FREE monthly Newsletter**
- ★ **Books available before they're in the shops**
- ★ **Exclusive Reader Service offers**

Accepting these FREE books and gift places you under no obligation to buy; you may cancel at any time, even after receiving your free shipment. Simply complete your details below and return the entire page to the address below. You don't even need a stamp!

YES! Please send me 4 free Modern Romance books and a surprise gift. I understand that unless you hear from me, I will receive 6 superb new titles every month for just £2.69 each, postage and packing free. I am under no obligation to purchase any books and may cancel my subscription at any time. The free books and gift will be mine to keep in any case.

P4ZEE

Ms/Mrs/Miss/Mr......................................Initials ....

BLOCK CAPITALS PLEASE

Surname ....

Address ....

....

....Postcode ....

Send this whole page to:

The Reader Service, FREEPOST CN81, Croydon, CR9 3WZ